SO WILLS THE

Heart

Corrissa James

ISBN: 0692384642

ISBN-13: 978-0692384640

Inkwell International

Laurel, NE 68745

www.inkwellinternational.com

SO WILLS THE

Heart

Chapter One

Evie Jacobson looked at the stack of boxes already packed up in her great aunt's farmhouse, then at all the stuff still left to sort through. She plopped down onto the couch, which she was sure was brought into the house when it was built some eight decades ago. She'd already been working for several days, but she could barely see any progress.

She never even knew this great aunt existed, so when the lawyer contacted her and explained that the childless widow had left everything to her, Evie was stunned. Even more shocking was that the bulk of the estate was a two-thousand square foot house on approximately twenty acres in the northern part of Nebraska. To Evie, it had to be a mistake. She had no family in Nebraska, and neither she nor her sister Liz had never even been to the state, but the lawyer insisted that everything checked out. Their great aunt was their grandmother's older half-sister.

The lawyer had offered to sell the property, lock, stock, and barrel, which he estimated to be worth about $200,000, and send her a check, but on a whim Evie decided it was just the break she needed. She was famous for her whims, so her sister was not surprised to learn of Evie's plan to drive from Denver to an area just south of the tiny town of Bender, Nebraska. Getting the time off work had been a bit tricky, but it helped that the boss had a soft spot for her.

"Out of one fire and into…a complete mess."

She flopped down on the sofa. Nebraska wasn't the escape she'd been hoping for. She'd expected chasing fireflies through fields of rolling hills and staring at the millions of stars in the sky until she fell asleep each night. Instead, she was trapped in a dusty house surrounded by overgrown weeds. Everywhere she looked she saw knickknacks, ranging from Hummel figurines to "as seen on TV" products. She never dreamed one woman could collect so much stuff. And now Evie was responsible for dealing with all of it. A feeling of claustrophobia crowded in on her, and Evie knew she had to get out of the house, escaping the dust and humidity for the day.

She jumped into her ancient Honda Accord and decided to go exploring around the countryside. She'd enjoy the violet chicory and bright yellow sweet clover dotting the roadside and perhaps even drive up to the Missouri River. She drove east along the gravel road until she hit the highway, but instead of turning to head toward civilization, she continued along the gravel road, singing along with the radio as she followed her whim, turning left or right along roads that promised adventure—or at least a change of pace.

Two hours later, she was hot, cranky, and completely lost. She could get no signal on her cell phone, and she hadn't seen an inhabited house for miles. She passed plenty of old houses that were caving in on themselves or had been turned into shelters for cows or wildlife, but the human population seemed to have vanished. Retracing the way she'd come wasn't much help as she hadn't been paying attention, just enjoying the freedom of a sunny day spent driving in a car.

She decided to head west until she ran into a highway or some other major road, but quickly came to a fork in the road, forcing her to choose south or north.

"Seriously? It's never easy, is it."

A cow in the field looked up and lowed in response. Evie stuck out her tongue, then finally turned north. Maybe she'd get to see the river today after all.

She traveled another two miles without passing a crossroad, and the road she was on was becoming increasingly difficult to maneuver. Deep ruts from tractors or rain or God-knew-what bounced her little car back and forth until Evie thought she might be experiencing whiplash. She looked for a place to turn around, but the road was alternatingly lined with deep ditches or sandy bluffs, both of which crowded the already narrow road, making it difficult to do a simple U-turn. Finally she saw a small lane heading off the road. A split log with a blackened arrow burnt into it pointed down the road.

Curious, she pulled in and followed the dirt road into a cluster of soaring cottonwoods, in the middle of which she found a small pond circled on one side by large boulders. The dirt road appeared to circle behind the boulders and come out on the other side, rejoining itself where she was parked. She turned off the car and listened for a moment, hearing nothing but the birds whistling in the trees. The pond seemed to call to her, and she walked to its edge, crouching to dip her fingers into the cool water. The water was amazingly clear—so clear that she could see the sandy bottom well out into the pond. If this was someone's private swimming hole, it was in the most secluded place possible. She wished she had thought to grab her bathing suit before leaving the house today.

"Although I am on vacation. What better time to be a little daring, right?"

She stripped off her clothes and waded into the cool water, feeling it embrace her and relax her muscles while washing away the grit of the day. The pond was deeper than she expected, and she was able to swim back and forth, stretching her arms out and releasing the tension from her back. She flipped over onto her back, staring up at the giant expanse of blue above her. In that moment, she felt a peace she hadn't experienced in years. In fact, she couldn't ever remember feeling so relaxed, so in tune with the world around her.

The few days she'd been away from home had already given her some perspective on her life in Denver, and she decided in that moment to quit her graphic design job. Her boss wouldn't be too happy, especially as he believed that they were heading toward an illicit affair.

Evie let the sun warm her face, her breasts, and any stretch of skin not covered by water.

She wasn't having an affair with him, although he had a manliness about him that most women would find attractive.

"The kind of manliness that can make a girl feel like a real woman."

She closed her eyes, picturing what just such a man would do to her. Soon a languid warmth spread throughout her that had nothing to do with the sun. She imagined him chuckling in her ear, a rich sound that sent waves of excitement fluttering throughout her body. She rolled her head slightly toward the sound, blinking lazily against the sun.

She saw the boulders, now closer than she expected. She blinked again, then saw deeply tanned muscular arms and a chest leading up to a head with dark hair. She smiled. Now here was the kind of man she could really become addicted to. He was holding one hand up in front of his face, his fingers splayed open slightly so he could see through them, although he was looking just off to the side.

"I just wanted to give you a heads up that I was here. Please don't scream."

But she was already screaming, suddenly remembering where she was, which was not in a bedroom with her boss, but naked in a pond, with her clothes on the far bank. She jerked forward, trying to turn away from the man while hugging her hands across her breasts.

"I wasn't looking, I swear." He stood up, the water coming to just above his waist, and did a slow circle as if to show he wasn't hiding anything. He chuckled, and it was the same rich chuckle that shook Evie to her toes. "Well, I wasn't staring. Not too much."

"Such chivalry." Her sarcasm elicited a full-on laugh.

Evie could feel her face burning, and she didn't think it was from the sun. She realized that even if she swam away, she would have to exit the water and walk fully naked to her car, where she'd left her clothes. She frowned. She wondered if he would be gentlemanly enough to turn around if she asked. She paddled around slightly so she could see him at the base of the largest rock.

"I don't suppose—"

"Nope." He smiled, and again Evie felt a shock to her toes. His good looks were quite captivating. "I've got a front row seat and I plan to enjoy it. You can't blame a man for enjoying a beautiful woman."

She looked from him to her car, then back again, trying to hide a smile. Why did his compliment make her practically giggly with delight? She knew nothing about him, but his now blatant staring, coupled with his charming honesty, was giving her a confidence that she decided was worth exploring.

"You aren't a mass murderer or anything like that?"

He shook his head. "Don't even enjoy hunting."

"And you're all alone? There's no one else who's going to pop up and announce themselves?"

"No, ma'am. Just me, myself, and I."

"This your land?"

He laughed again. "No, certainly not."

"So you're trespassing."

"Just like you."

"Are you from around here?"

"Are you a journalist?"

She shook her head.

"Because you sure do ask a lot of questions."

She shrugged. "I like to know what I am dealing with."

He smiled. "Oh, so you're dealing with me now, eh?"

"Well, I was thinking about it." The response popped out of her mouth before she considered what she was saying. The transformation in him was instantaneous. The muscles in his chest tightened, and his sky blue eyes darkened to a deep sapphire.

"I'm going to swim out into the water a bit. No screaming, okay?"

His voice sent pleasurable shivers down her spine, and her mouth went dry. She couldn't scream if her life depended on it.

He stopped when he was about five feet from her, and they both stared at each other while treading water, although Evie kept one arm wrapped around her chest. She told herself it was stupid to be bashful at this point, especially as she couldn't cover her entire body and the water was clear enough to see anything.

"My God, you're beautiful. If you're some kind of water nymph here to seduce me to my death, I give. I'm all yours."

The sincerity in his voice emboldened her, and she swept both arms out to her sides as she turned to face him, giving him a full view of her body. His sharp intake of breath was the most sensual sound she'd ever heard. She moved a little closer to him, letting her gaze travel its own path. She paused to study his lips, licking her own as she imagined the taste of his kisses. Then her gaze dropped lower to his broad chest and down until she could see, through the water, the patch of hair leading down from his navel. Her eyes flew up to his face, and she blushed when she realized he'd been watching her take in the sights.

He brought a hand up out of the water and extended it over to her. "Jonathan Clark."

She giggled at his formality and stuck her hand out to his. "Evelyn Jacobson, but everyone calls me Evie."

He squeezed her hand gently, but didn't let go. Instead, he pulled her through the water until she was pressed against his chest. She should have been terrified, letting this strange man hold her so closely that wherever their skin touched it screamed in desire, but his embrace was tender, a caress like nothing she'd ever felt. She felt no fear with him except the fear that he wouldn't kiss her, wouldn't press his body more tightly against hers, wouldn't bring her the sweet release that she craved so badly.

He held her, but did nothing more, and she realized that he was waiting for her. *You started this, Evie. Do you have the courage to see it through?* She bit her bottom lip, and she felt him moan as she slid her arms around his neck, pulling herself against him even more tightly to wrap her legs around his waist. He held her waist as he buried his face in her neck and she arched into him, lifting her head back to give him full access to her neck while pressing her breasts into his chest. He dropped his hands to her buttocks, kneading them in the water as he pulled her closer. His lips teased across her collarbone. His head dipped lower, but the water prevented him from reaching his real target. He growled, holding Evie tight against him with one hand as he used the other to propel them closer to shore.

Just as his feet hit the sandy bottom, they both heard the honking. He stopped walking, still holding her wrapped around his body, the water now barely reaching his waist. They both looked toward the gravel road, listening to the honking. It was definitely getting closer.

"Son of a bitch!" He pushed her toward the shore. "Go on, get dressed and get going before they get here."

She stopped and turned back to him, the water lapping at her knees. His darkened gaze traveled the full length of her completely exposed body, making Evie feel as if she'd been ravaged by a most pleasurable lover. He finally looked her in the eye.

"It's been nice meeting you, Evelyn Jacobson."

"You too, Jonathan Clark."

She raced up the bank and to her car, throwing on her t-shirt and shorts without bothering with her underwear. She started the car just as a truck arrived. The man driving looked oddly familiar. She caught one last glimpse of Jonathan as he slipped between two of the boulders, realizing that the new arrival had his same coloring. *Brothers?* She wasn't sticking around to find out. She drove down the lane and back to the gravel road, laughing in disbelief at her audacity.

"Well, that's one way to meet new people, Evie."

Chapter Two

Jonathan made it back to the boulders before the truck parked at the edge of the pond. As he pulled on his jeans, he was kicking himself for letting his sister Susannah know he was going swimming at Porters' pond for the afternoon. He'd recognized the sound of Daniel's truck powering down the lane, his brother appearing hell-bent on getting to the pond. Jonathan pulled his t-shirt on over his still-wet skin and scrambled over the boulder. He heard the splashing before he saw his brother in the water.

"Just what do you think you're doing?" Jonathan bellowed the question with as much authority as he could muster given that he was trying not to laugh at the same time.

Daniel whipped around to find the source of the sound, his eyes wide. When he saw Jonathan standing on the boulder, he smiled with relief and swam closer. "Jesus, Jonathan! You about made me shit myself, thinking old man Porter was out here with his shotgun again."

This time Jonathan couldn't stop the laughter. "Again?"

"He was freaking out because me and Alex were out here skinny dipping last week."

Jonathan whistled. "Alex Porter?"

Daniel frowned up at his brother. "Yes, Alex Porter. What other Alex would I mean?"

"Well, lemme see." Jonathan pretended to think for a moment.

Daniel splashed water up at him. "Fine, what other Alexandria would I mean?"

Jonathan side-stepped the splashing without getting wet, although he almost lost his balance on the boulder in the process.

"I'm actually supposed to be meeting her out here today," Daniel said.

"You too?" Jonathan laughed again as Daniel's eyes tightened and his face reddened, then held up his hands in mock surrender. "I'm kidding!"

"You'd better be. I thought that was her car when I pulled up."

"No such luck, brother."

Daniel swam a bit closer. "Wait, so I'm not the only one doing a little skinny dipping at the pond?"

Jonathan remembered watching Evie floating on her back in the cool water, the sunlight washing over her breasts. Suddenly he was annoyed at his brother's intrusion, interrupting his tryst with his very own water nymph. "I took a quick dip to cool off, but I was alone."

Daniel's derisive snort irritated Jonathan further. He didn't want his older brother to concern himself with what he and Evie had been doing—or almost doing.

Jonathan crossed his arms. "So what do you think Lucas is going to do when he finds us both gone?"

Daniel's smile disappeared, and he swore loudly. "I figured you were still out with the cattle, that you'd cover for me."

With their brother Andrew serving thirty days in the county jail for vandalism of the neighbor's ranch and Lucas, the eldest Clark brother, working part-time on the same ranch to help heal the rift between the two families, Jonathan and Daniel were left to take care of the entire farm, including their one hundred head of cattle. Their sister, Susannah, was supposed to help out too, but Jonathan had noticed her sneaking out late at night on more than one occasion. Her mind was elsewhere, and he wasn't about to ruin her chance of blowing off a little steam. Lord knew she'd earned it, having to deal with four older brothers. However, Daniel was another story. He'd interrupted Jonathan's unexpected encounter with Evie, and for that, his brother would have to pay.

Luckily the opportunity presented itself when another car raced down the lane. Daniel waved from the water, then turned back to Jonathan.

"Man, you've gotta help me out." When Jonathan didn't respond, Daniel resorted to begging. "C'mon! It's Alexandria Porter!"

Jonathan watched Alex get out of her car and stretch, as if she'd been driving for hours instead of a few minutes. Alexandria Porter was the stuff of teenage boys' fantasies—as well as the fantasies of quite a few grown men. She was what his sister described as voluptuous. To look at her, Alex practically oozed sex. The fact that she was one of the sweetest girls in the area—and that her mother had been his mother's best friend—created a disconnect for Jonathan. He could certainly understand why men were attracted to her, but to him she was like a cousin. Daniel, however, had no such misgivings.

"Jonathan, man, please. I'm begging you!"

Jonathan hesitated just long enough for his brother to squirm. "Fine, but you owe me one."

"Anything, man. Anything!"

Daniel swam to the far edge, staying in the water as he spoke to Alex. He pointed to Jonathan on the boulders, and Alex shielded her eyes against the afternoon sun, then waved at him as she called out a greeting across the pond. He waved back before sliding off the back side of the boulder, crawling into his truck, and driving out from behind the boulders, stopping to talk to Alex.

"Hey, Johnny." She leaned through the open window to give him a quick peck.

"Hey, sweetcheeks." He could see Daniel in the water behind her, the disgruntled look plastered on his face once again.

Alex batted Jonathan playfully on the shoulder. "If you've got a few minutes, stop up and see Mom. She'd love to see you at least once this summer."

"You sure? She's not gonna pull your dad's shotgun on me, is she?"

Alex rolled her eyes than glanced back at Daniel, whose face turned even redder. "He told you about that, huh? Yeah, Dad was ready to ground me until I'm thirty."

"You must've sweet talked him pretty good to be out in public again so soon."

She smoothed her hands back and forth along the window frame, trying to hide the smile that was spreading across her face.

"Alexandria Porter! Did you sneak out of your house?"

She rolled her eyes, but her grin grew even larger.

"And all for Daniel, huh? He's one lucky son of a gun." He reached over to hold her chin, making her look at him. "You just make him treat you right, understand?"

She nodded.

"And if he doesn't, you let me know."

She giggled. "Pretty sure he could take you, Johnny."

Jonathan shrugged. "Fair enough. But I got Lucas on my side."

"Don't worry. Danny's been a real gentleman."

Jonathan leaned to look over her shoulder at his brother. "We are talking about Daniel Clark, right?"

She batted his shoulder again. "Go on, get out of here, you cad. And don't forget to stop by Mom's."

He nodded, then yelled out loud enough for Daniel to hear, "I'll make sure your dad knows where you're at." He laughed when he saw his brother's eyes grow wide, then waved and drove down the lane.

When he got to the main road, he paused, wondering which way Evie Jacobson had gone. Why hadn't he gotten a phone number or address—something? He didn't know any Jacobsons, so he didn't think she was from around here. Had she even been real? He remembered the taste of her salty neck and the feeling of her legs wrapped around him.

If she wasn't real, she was the best damn fantasy he'd ever had.

Chapter Three

Evie drove north along the same gravel road that had led her to the not-so-secret pond. About a mile from the lane, when she was just out of sight of it, she pulled along the edge of the road to wait and see if Jonathan would follow her. Surely he would see the dust that her car had kicked up. Even now, nearly ten minutes after she turned onto the road, the air was hazy all around her. But no one passed her on the road, and she realized that she was meant to have only a fleeting moment, a memory of her wild youth that she would recall fondly one day. Too bad she didn't get to see it through to the end. She had no doubt that Jonathan Clark knew how to pleasure a woman.

She drove several more miles before she finally came to a paved road. She headed west, hoping she would find something familiar or a sign pointing her back to her great aunt's house. Fifteen minutes later, and after doubling back several times when she ran into dead ends, she drove through a small town that consisted of a permanently closed gas station, several abandoned buildings, and a bar that had two neon signs flashing in the window: DINER and OPEN. The parking lot was empty.

Inside, she found a long counter with low stools attached to the floor. Opposite the counter, and along the blacked out windows, was a row of several booths. At the far end of the room she saw a pool table and several chairs. She didn't see any people.

"Hello?" She waited for a response. "Anybody here?" She looked backed toward where the kitchen should be, whispering, "Anybody who isn't going to kill me?"

A door slammed at the far end of the room, and Evie jerked toward the sound. A tall older woman wearing a stained apron was walking toward her.

"Sit wherever you like." The woman's face was streaked with sweat.

"Actually, I—"

"I'll bring you water and a menu. Just give me a second to put this knucklehead in his place."

She walked through a swinging door into the kitchen and immediately started yelling something about not interfering in "her" life. A male voice responded that "she" would do what he said as long as she lived under his roof. That was all Evie heard as the voices disappeared into some unseen area.

She sat down on one of the stools and waited. She checked her phone. No messages. No data service either. She could pull up a map using one of her apps, but the GPS service couldn't track her location. The Internet wouldn't load.

"Great. Stuck in a bar, but I don't know where."

"It's the Porterhouse."

She swung around on the stool to see Jonathan Clark standing just inside the doorway.

He smiled. "Can't get enough of me, huh?"

"Oh, you can help me! Where am I?"

"Porterhouse Bar."

"No, I mean what city."

He frowned, then cocked his head. "Excuse me?"

She slid off the stool, laughing at his expression as she moved to show him the map on her phone. "I'm visiting the area and went out exploring today, kinda got lost. This is where I need to be." She held up the phone, but he ignored it.

"Visiting, huh? I guessed as much." He pushed past her to walk behind the bar, where he filled a red plastic cup with ice and water from a soda dispenser. He drank the entire cup without pausing, never taking his eyes off her. He refilled the empty cup and handed it to her. He leaned both elbows on the counter, then looked up at her as she drank. When his eyes dropped to her neck, she nearly choked on the water. He looked back up at her and smiled.

"You sure you're just visiting? Couldn't you at least pretend to be thinking of staying?"

She shrugged and set the plastic cup down on the bar. "I could see myself living out here, with all the open skies." She caught her breath. What made her say that? She hadn't even considered leaving Denver to live here, but when she looked at Jonathan, who was watching her closely, she smiled. Yes, she could see herself enjoying afternoon swims with him. "Actually, I am here cleaning out my great aunt's house. She left it to me, along with a little money, so I thought I might quit my job and move out into the country and work on my art for a while, see if I can develop it into a career." She heard the words coming from her mouth, but had no idea where they were coming from.

"So do it."

"Which part?"

"All of it."

She sighed. "Unfortunately, it's not that simple."

"Sure it is." He moved around the bar to sit on a stool next to her, his arm and shoulder so close to her own that she could feel the heat emanating from them. She fought the urge to throw him on the counter and finish what they had started at the pond. "Which part is the hardest?"

"Well, I already have the house, and the money is in a bank account."

"What about your house back in...?"

"In Denver? Actually all my stuff's in storage. I decided to move to a bigger apartment once I got the money from my great aunt, but haven't found one yet."

"So all that's left is quitting your job."

She rolled her eyes. "Oh, is that all?"

"How hard can it be? Just call them up and say 'I quit.'"

"Let's just say it's complicated."

He was silent for a moment, studying her. Then he leaned over to nudge her. "So text message instead of calling them?"

She giggled. "That would be easier."

He swiveled around on the stool to look at her. "So what are you waiting for, Evie Jacobson, my little water nymph?"

He was teasing her, and she knew it, but she also saw the glimmer of hope in his eyes. He wanted her to be daring. *Just like the girl at the pond.*

Could she? She chewed on her lip and tried to think rationally, but his closeness made her thoughts scatter in all directions.

"Evie?"

"Yeah?"

He leaned toward her, until he was just inches from her face. Evie found it hard to breath.

"If you don't quit chewing on your lip, I am going to make love to you on this counter."

She turned bright red when she realized that they were both thinking about having wild, uncontrollable sex. Before she realized what she was doing, she had typed out the text on her phone. She re-read it, making sure it sounded appropriate, but Jonathan dropped his hand to her knee and, once again, all her thoughts scattered. When he started sliding his hand up and down her thigh, she laughed nervously.

"You're making it impossible to concentrate."

"Oh, sorry." He shifted his hand to her inner thigh, sliding his hand up her leg and into her shorts.

Evie jumped off the stool as his eyes widened. She backed away from him, but within two steps he had her pinned against the wall. She could think of nowhere she'd rather be. His eyes were smoldering, and he pressed his body in until they were barely touching. She desperately wished he'd move closer. Her body was screaming at being so close to what it wanted—needed—but not being satisfied.

"I can't control myself if you're going to go commando."

She tried to turn away from him, but he pulled her chin back so she was forced to look in his eyes.

"It wasn't planned, you know." Her legs felt like wet noodles, and she knew that if he weren't standing so close, she'd slide to the floor.

He dropped his face in toward her neck, but once again he got as close to her skin as possible without actually touching her. He moved from her neck to her collarbone, then back up to her ear, his hot breath leaving goose bumps in their wake.

"Jonathan, please."

"Do you want me?"

She felt the breath rush from her. "In the worst way."

"Send the text, Evie."

She lifted her hand, realizing she still held the phone. She hit send. There was no hesitation in her decision this time. She looked back to him. "Done."

"Make sure it went through, because once I start, I don't think I will be able to stop."

She smiled when she saw the tightness in his mouth. He was barely keeping himself in control. She watched the "sending" signal on her phone spin round and round. Finally she turned the screen toward him. "Done."

"Thank God."

Chapter Four

"Jonathan Michael Clark, just what do you think you're doing?"

Jonathan scowled, his lips just inches from Evie's. He closed his eyes, struggling to regain control. Why was the world conspiring against him? What had he done to deserve such torture? He opened his eyes and pulled back from Evie just enough that he wouldn't be yelling in her face. "Go away, *Mom*!"

Evie slapped her hand over her mouth to keep from laughing.

"Oh, you'll pay for that," he hissed at her playfully.

The female voice behind him snorted. "Your dear mother is probably rolling over in her grave right now given the way you're speaking to me in my own bar—and manhandling my customers! Let the poor girl order."

"She's not hungry."

"Nonsense! Let her go, already."

Evie stood on her tiptoes to look over Jonathan's shoulder. "Actually, I'm not hungry. I just stopped in for directions."

The woman harrumphed loudly. "Fine, fine, Jonathan, give her what she wants."

"With pleasure."

Evie burst out laughing, clinging to Jonathan's shoulder as tears ran down her cheeks.

"Oh, yes, because this is just the kind of reaction a man wants from a woman."

"I'm sorry." Evie gasped between laughs. "It's just too ridiculous to believe."

Jonathan stepped back from her and ran a hand through his dark hair. "I've never had this much trouble kissing a woman."

"Kissed a lot of them, have you?"

He winked at her. "Enough to know that they're nothing compared to you."

"Wow." She fanned herself with her hand. "You definitely know what to say to get the blood boiling."

He ran his thumb along her bottom lip. "Oh, just you wait, Evie Jacobson."

Her phone blared to life, and Evie lifted it to see who was calling. He noted the shakiness in her hand and relaxed a bit. At least he wasn't the only one affected so powerfully.

She groaned, then tapped a button on the phone and looked back to him.

"Let me guess. The ex-boss?"

"Ex-boss, ex everything." She waved a hand at Jonathan's frown, as if brushing away the comment. "Since I apparently now live in Nebraska. Although I still don't know where exactly."

"Okay, okay, show me the map." He shifted to stand behind her, his hands on her shoulders as she pulled up the map on her phone. "Can you zoom out a bit?" He dropped his left hand down over her shoulder to point to the mark on the map. "You live here, yes?"

She nodded.

"Hmm, I think I know where that is." He pulled his hand back to cup her left breast, kneading it gently. "But I'll only tell you if you make me a promise."

Evie pretended to push away his hand, but when he loosened his hold, she pulled her elbows to her side, trapping his hand in place. "What's that?"

"You'll always go commando for me." He squeezed her nipple until the hardened nub pressed through her thin t-shirt.

She collapsed back against him. "I promise. I'll promise anything if you just keep doing what you're doing."

He abruptly pulled his hand from her breast and stepped back, causing Evie to stumble as she tried to regain her footing. "All right, then. Let's get you home."

The phone vibrated in Evie's hand while playing a *ding-ding-ding* that signaled a new text message. Jonathan swiped it from her hand.

"Hey!" She reached for the phone, but he held it above his head. "Come on, not funny."

He watched her try and jump for it, rubbing up and down against him in the process. "No, not funny." He was staring at the two pert nubs pushing through the thin fabric of her t-shirt and wondering what Ma Porter would do if she came back out to find him ripping off Evie's clothes.

Evie realized he was staring at her chest and crossed her arms tightly.

Jonathan sighed loudly and handed her phone back to her, affecting a pout. "You take all my fun away."

As he escorted her out to her car, her phone rang. Jonathan wanted to grab it from her hands and throw it out on the highway, smashing it to a million pieces, but he was pretty sure that would sent the wrong message. The fact that she ignored the ringing gave him hope, though.

"He's persistent, huh?"

"You have no idea."

He opened her car door and waited for her to slide in behind the steering wheel. Leaning into to the car he asked, "Is this something I need to worry about, Evie?"

His brows furrowed together. She reached out to caress his cheek. "No, absolutely not."

"You sure? Because I don't do the whole casual dating thing." At least not with her. Never with her. He couldn't stomach the thought of sharing her with any man. He stepped back and closed her door, trying to put some distance between them before he caused a scene in the parking lot. What was it about her that made him want to lose control?

"Oh, so we're dating now? You move awfully quickly, Mr. Clark."

He leaned against the door to reach in and pull her hand to his mouth. He kissed the palm, running the tip of his tongue back and forth. "You did just quit your job for me."

"True."

Her breathy response aroused Jonathan more than he cared to admit, and he moved his lips to the inside of her wrist, caressing it with his tongue.

She whimpered. "So we're dating."

He looked up from his assault on her wrist. "At the very least."

Chapter Five

Evie was disappointed when Jonathan didn't escort her home, especially as she ended up spending the entire thirty-minute drive imagining everything he might have done to her—and what she would have done to him. Instead, he had pointed down the road, given her directions to get back to a highway she recognized, then watched her drive away. It was only when she got home that she realized she had not given him her phone number or address.

Her frustration from the day made it impossible to sleep that night. But she decided that she couldn't go back to the bar to find him again. She simply could not suffer through any more of his advances only to leave unfulfilled. She'd just chalk him up as a happy memory, as she had originally planned to do.

Except she had quit her job because of him.

Living in Nebraska was not part of her long-term plan. She rolled her eyes. "Not that I have a long-term plan."

But why couldn't it be? A fresh start, a secluded hideaway, and enough money to live for at least a year…if she was prudent with her money, she might get two years out of it. She could focus on building her client base, whether through galleries or individuals. And she could always teach private courses. A picture of her future was taking shape rather nicely.

Her decision to give Nebraska a go, coupled with her need to put Jonathan firmly out of her mind, resulted in a newfound energy that she focused on the house. She tackled the upstairs first, packing and sorting through the bedrooms. Halfway through the first day of the invigorated purge, she dragged the mattresses out into the hallway and dismantled the bed frames.

"And you just think about what you've done to deserve this punishment." She wagged a finger at the mattresses. "Putting those nasty thoughts into my head of what Jonathan would do to me if he were here. I'll have none of that. I'll just crash on the sofa until you can learn to control yourself."

She also turned her cell phone to vibrate. The persistence of Nathan, her boss—ex-boss, she reminded herself—was reaching new levels, and every time the phone sounded her heart jumped, thinking it was Jonathan, even though she knew he didn't have her phone number.

At the end of her second day of working upstairs, she had completely emptied the three rooms, whose windows looked primarily to the south and west. She decided that the largest of the rooms would make the perfect studio, so after another night of practically non-existent sleep, she drove to Omaha to shop the art supply stores for brushes, canvases, and paint. She also picked up wall paint to cover up the dreary neutral tan her great aunt had used throughout the house. Evie chose rich yellows and peaches, hoping she could bring some life to the walls while highlighting the house's natural wood floors.

She didn't notice the bouquet of wildflowers sitting on the porch until the third trip to unload the car, and when she finally did see them, she screamed so loudly that she startled the birds in the giant oak trees surrounding the house. There was no note, but they had to be from Jonathan. The only other person who knew she was here was the lawyer, and she had a sneaking suspicion that he was in his seventies based on how his voice crackled through the phone. She placed the flowers in one her great aunt's pitchers since she couldn't find any vases, then placed them on the center of the kitchen table.

That night she fell asleep just as her head hit the pillow—and woke up just as quickly. If Jonathan dropped the flowers off, then he knew where she lived. The thought reopened all sorts of possibilities, and she tossed and turned most of the night. She told herself it was because of the uncomfortable sofa, but no matter how many times she said it, she couldn't get the voice in her head to stop laughing at her. Finally, around 4 a.m. she got up and stormed into the kitchen. She grabbed the flowers off the table and headed up to her new studio, where she recreated the flowers in watercolors on one of her canvases. The sun was well above the horizon by the time she was satisfied with what she had done, and she set the canvas aside to dry.

When she returned to the kitchen, now desperate for coffee, she realized that it was almost 11 a.m. She was debating whether to make the coffee or go back to bed when a knock sounded on her door.

"Hey, sleepyhead."

Evie pulled her robe around her tightly, suddenly self-conscious about how she looked.

Jonathan chuckled. "Don't worry, I still think you're beautiful, but hurry and get dressed."

She tried to feign disinterest, but she was pretty sure was failing miserably as she couldn't help but let her eyes wander over his muscular physique.

"I have been appointed as your 'welcome to the community' ambassador and am here to give you your official tour."

"You're joking."

He shrugged. "Well, I'm here, so get dressed and let's go." He started down the steps to his truck, then turned back. "And Evie?"

"Yeah?"

"Remember, commando. You promised."

She closed the door, her face hot with embarrassment, then raced to get dressed—sans underwear, but she wasn't going all day without a bra. She pulled her hair back into a ponytail and was out in the truck within ten minutes of Jonathan's arrival. He nodded in approval as he steered the truck down the lane and out onto the country road.

"How did you know where I lived? I never told you my aunt's name."

Jonathan grabbed her hand and kissed it. "It's the country. We all know everybody here."

"Then why'd you wait three days to come visit me?"

"I was waiting for you to make the next move."

"Oh really?"

"Yep."

"Stop the truck."

"What's wrong?"

"Stop the truck—now!"

He swerved onto the shoulder and put the truck in park before turning to her. "What's wrong?"

She slid across the seat, crawled onto his lap, and straddled him before grabbing his face and pulling him into a kiss unlike anything she'd ever done before. It was both intoxicating and demanding, passionate and tender. She felt an overpowering desire to tear off all his clothes and an equally powerful desire to hold him close, keeping him all to herself. When she thought she couldn't survive another possible second of his tongue and lips claiming hers, she pulled away and slid off his lap.

"So how was that for a move?"

Jonathan stared straight ahead, his hands clenching the steering wheel. He nodded without looking at her. "That'll do." He started the truck, pulled out onto the road, then whipped a U-turn and headed back to her house.

"What about the—?"

"Tour's over. Nothing to see here anyway."

They drove back to the house, Evie laughing the entire way, but Jonathan had the last laugh. He turned off the truck and before Evie could get out of the passenger side, he grabbed her hand. "One favor, please."

She rolled her eyes. "Now what?"

"Can you show me that move again?"

She climbed back across his lap. "You, sir, ask for some of the best favors." Instead of kissing him like before, she focused her attention on his neck, doing to him what he had done to her in the bar the other day, moving from his ear to his throat and back again, never actually touching his skin with her lips. He gripped her hips and shifted her slightly on his lap, making more room for his now obvious excitement. Evie smiled, letting her tongue dart out first to his earlobe, then to the base of his throat.

She pulled back to look down at him through heavily lidded eyes. "How's that?"

"Maybe show me just one more time."

She slapped him playfully on the chest and tried to slide off his lap, but he flipped her around to lay her down on the seat and moved his body to pin her down. "My turn."

He unleashed his tongue, letting it dance across her lips until she whimpered, then he let her tangle her own tongue around his, pulling it into her mouth. He kissed her so deeply Evie thought she might pass out from the waves of desire he was creating through her body. When she was finally ready to give in to the fire within her, letting it consume her, he shifted away from her mouth to her shoulder, pulling down her t-shirt to explore the flesh there. He kissed all long her neckline, never dipping below it. She wanted to tear off her shirt and expose her breasts to his magic tongue, but every time she moved to pull her shirt off, he grabbed her hands and held them away. He pushed them above her head, then lifted his eyes to look into hers. "Behind your head."

She pouted, but complied. Placing her hands behind her head prevented her from exploring his body the way he was exploring hers, but it did create a natural arch in her back, thrusting her breasts even higher into the air.

He slid his hands under her shirt, lifting it to expose her stomach. He kissed her, tickling her in a way that made her giggle and groan with pleasure at the same time. He moved up closer to her breasts. Evie held her breath as he hands slid further up her shirt to cup both breasts. She nearly cried when he jerked them back and sat up, pulling her shirt up to reveal her bra. He frowned. "This is not what we agreed to."

She dropped her hands and pulled down her shirt. "You have got to be kidding." She slid out from under him and opened the passenger door.

"You promised, Evie."

She stepped out of the truck, but before she closed the door behind her, she pulled down the side of her shorts, revealing that she wasn't wearing any panties. "And I delivered." She turned and raced into the house, giggling at the growling that was following after her just as quickly.

Chapter Six

Jonathan bounded out of the truck and across the yard, but he was not fast enough to catch Evie, who slammed the door in his face. He heard the deadbolt just as he reached for the handle. He stood on the front porch for a moment, trying to figure her out. He hadn't been able to get Evie out of his head for the last few days, no matter how much he tried—and he'd tried. He'd not only done his own chores on the farm, but also those of his brothers Daniel and Andrew. When he'd offered to help his sister, she'd asked him what was wrong.

The truth was, nothing was wrong, except that he knew he had to find Evie again. The fearlessness she'd displayed at the pond and again at the bar—he had to get to know this woman better!

"Evelyn Jacobson, you open this door right now!" When she didn't respond, he shifted tactics, from pretending to demand to all-out begging. "Please, Evie."

He twisted the door handle, but the door didn't budge. He rested his forehead against the thick wooden door.

"Evie, Evie, let me in."

She giggled from the other side of the door. "Not by the hair of my chinny chin chin."

"Ew, chin hair?" Jonathan feigned a sound of disgust. "Sorry, I don't do chicks with facial hair. That's just...ew!"

He was trying not to laugh when she threw open the door, the scowl on her face indicating that she was ready to do battle. Before she could stop him, he stepped inside, closing the door behind him. He leaned against the door. "Listen, about that chin hair. I'm sure you can do electrolysis or maybe have it bleached."

She rolled her eyes at him. "Seriously, get out of my house."

"What's the matter? Afraid to deliver what you promised?" He stepped closer to her, fighting to control himself. He didn't think she'd scare easily, but he didn't want to test that boundary. Not yet.

She didn't back down. "I didn't promise anything." She jutted her chin out, as if that was all the proof she needed.

Jonathan squinted, turning his head to the side. He pointed at her chin. "Chin hair!"

She knocked his hand away and laughed at him. "Oh give it up, already."

He grabbed her hand and pulled it to his chest. "Never." He winked and gave her a toothy grin.

Evie looked away, tugging her hand away.

"Hey, there. Wait a minute." He bent down slightly and shifted until he was in her line of sight of again. When she looked elsewhere, he moved again. He continued moving with her, following her into the living room. Finally, she couldn't hold back her smile any longer. "Ah, there's my little water nymph. Everything okay?"

"Yeah, I just..." She shrugged. She opened one of numerous brown boxes, pretending to be focused on its contents.

Jonathan finally took a large step back from her. "Ah, lemme guess. A commitment-phobe?"

"Guilty as charged."

He nodded. "I get it. You need your space. Your wish is my command." He bowed deeply. When he glanced up at her, she was covering her mouth to hide her giggles. He wanted to pull her hand away and become intoxicated by her laughter. "So I guess that means we're back to the city tour?"

"Ugh, no!" Evie held up both hands and shook her head. "I've got better things to do with my time."

"Like me?"

She flashed a smile over her shoulder. "Maybe."

He clasped both hands to his chest, as if he'd been shot in the heart, then fell back on the sofa, pretending to die. It was one of his finest performances—or at least might have been had something not started vibrating under him. He reached down to find a cell phone. "Yours, I take it?"

She grabbed the phone, looked at the screen, then groaned. "My sister." She sat down on the sofa next to him. "This should be interesting."

Jonathan put his arm on the back of the sofa, and Evie sat back, dropping her free hand on his knee. It was a position that felt strangely comfortable, as if they'd known each other for far longer than a few days. It was a feeling he could definitely get used to, although he realized he probably shouldn't mention that to Evie.

"Hey, Liz." Evie looked at Jonathan and rolled her eyes.

She listened for a few moments, and Jonathan could hear the voice on the other end, although he couldn't make out what it was saying.

"Look, now's not a good time." Evie tugged at the seam on Jonathan's jeans with her fingernail. "Because. The city's welcoming committee is here and I—" She sat forward. "Yes, I'm staying." She stood up to pace in front of the sofa. "Look, I've made my decision. You'll just have to live with it." She glanced at Jonathan, then turned her back to him. "Fine, whatever."

She hung up and threw the phone in the open box. She followed it with several figurines, which she tossed into the box from several feet away. Jonathan cringed when he heard glass breaking.

"So, how's the family?" He thought the question had sounded playfully sarcastic, but when Evie turned to scowl in response, Jonathan held up his hands. "Okay, okay, no questions about the family."

"No, it's not that." Evie dropped her head and let her shoulders sag for a moment. "She's just..." She looked up and shrugged. "She's just all about babies right now. She's been trying to get pregnant like, forever, and it's all she talks about."

Jonathan leaned back, holding both hands to his head. "Ugh, babies. That puts a damper on the whole moment, doesn't it?" He heard Evie giggling, so he shifted slightly to be able to see her. "You think it's funny to torture me, don't you?"

"No, it's not that. I'm just glad you're not one of those people." She walked past him to the kitchen.

"One of what people?"

Evie stuck her head back in the living room. "You know. 'Oh, you'll like babies when you have your own.'"

"They could be right, I guess."

She frowned at him.

"Not that I want to find out, mind you."

"I'm making some iced tea. You want a glass?"

He nodded.

She went back into the kitchen just as the phone started vibrating again, shaking the large brown box.

"Hey, your phone's ringing again. Well, vibrating."

Evie called out over the sound of running water. "It's probably just Liz again. Just hit ignore, okay?"

Jonathan dug the phone out of the box and glanced at the screen. "It says Nathan." When she didn't respond, he yelled louder. "It's Nathan." When she still didn't respond, Jonathan answered the phone. "Hi, Evie's busy right—"

"Who is this?" Nathan's voice was clipped and hushed.

"Friend of Evie's here. Like I said, she's—"

"Friend? What friend?"

"Look, maybe I better give the phone to Evie."

"Listen, I don't know who you are, friend." Nathan practically snarled the word. "But understand that Evie has a life here in Denver, and it doesn't include you."

"Who are you talking to?" Evie stood in the doorway, holding two glasses of iced tea.

Jonathan held out the phone to her. "Some Nathan. I tried to—"

"Hang up."

He shrugged and did as he was told. "Dare I ask?"

"No." She handed him one of the glasses.

They drank the tea in silence, both standing uncomfortably by the table.

Finally, he set his glass down. "Look, I can handle a commitment-phobe, but I don't mess with another man's woman."

Evie choked on her tea, coughing several times. "He's not my man, and I am certainly not his woman."

"Oh, sorry. It just sounded—well, he talked like—"

"He's my boss."

"Oh." Jonathan tried to smile, but he knew it looked as fake as it felt. "Um, do I want to know what your job was? Because this guy seems awfully...determined to keep you under his control."

"Tell me about it." She sat on the sofa. "He's in love with me."

Chapter Seven

Evie focused on her hands, afraid to look up. She wasn't sure why she said it, she'd never told anyone. Not that she had those feelings for her boss. Nor had she ever encouraged them in any way. Yet she still felt...unclean.

She wanted Jonathan to say something. Actually, she wanted him to sit next to her so she could rest her head on his shoulder. No more talk about her life in Denver. Her *past* life. For now, she just wanted to enjoy the moment with Jonathan.

But the longer the silence continued, the more she saw the moment slipping away.

Finally, she glanced up at him, but he was looking out the window. "Jonathan?" She said it so quietly she didn't think he heard her. She cleared her throat. When he turned to look at her, she couldn't read his expression.

"I'm really attracted to you Evie. I mean, so attracted it hurts."

Evie remained silent, hoping this wasn't leading to a "but."

"I've never met anyone as fearless as you."

She blinked. "Fearless?"

"Yeah." He smiled and waved at the house around them. "Who else would quit their job and move to a new place like you did?"

She looked at him sideways. "Well, I kinda had inspiration for the quitting the job part."

"Do you love him?"

The question was so sudden, it took her breath away. She stuttered before finally yelling, "No!"

He moved to stand right in front of her, his knees almost touching hers as he looked down at her. "Are you sure? Are you sure you're not running away from something, maybe some feeling? Because I have to wonder."

She tried to stand up, but she couldn't with him standing so close. "Trust me. There is nothing going on there."

He stared at her for several long moments, and Evie could barely breathe. But she wouldn't look away, wouldn't break eye contact with him. She'd meant what she said, and she felt compelled to make sure he knew it.

"So that was no to the city tour because—what was it?—oh, yeah, 'better things to do with your time.' Care to enlighten me?"

Trying to catch up to his sudden shift, she blurted out the first thing that came to mind. "I need to paint the house."

He frowned as he walked to the front door.

"No, the inside. I need to paint inside."

Jonathan look relieved. "Want some help?"

They finished the two smaller upstairs rooms without much conversation. Jonathan hadn't even asked about the mattresses stacked up in the hallway. Evie couldn't look at them without remembering the thoughts they inspired—thoughts she was afraid that Jonathan would read all too easily on her face.

It was already dark outside when they moved to the final and largest room. Jonathan picked up the watercolor painting that she'd finished that morning and stared at it for several moments.

"It's beautiful." He nodded his appreciation. "You draw much?"

"Not enough. I mostly work on computers anymore. Well, I did." She chewed on her lip. "Now?" She shrugged.

"Draw me."

She hesitated, trying to come up with a reason to refuse, but her mind was coming up blank. "Okay."

She went downstairs to get one of the sketch pads she'd purchased in Omaha, along with a variety of pencils. On a whim, she grabbed a few of the candles she'd found while packing up the house. She'd argue that they were for better lighting, if he asked.

When she returned to the studio, Jonathan had moved two of the mattresses into the room and was pulling off his t-shirt.

"Um, what are you doing there, cowboy?"

"You're gonna draw me nude." He cut her off before she could protest. "It's not like we haven't seen each other naked already."

"If this is a come on, you really don't have to work so hard." Her heart was beating so loudly she was sure he could hear it.

He walked over to stand in front of her. "If this were a come on, you'd already be naked." He took the candles from her.

"Fair point."

As she organized her pencils and prepped the sketchpad, Jonathan lit the candles and placed them around the mattress. When she turned back to the mattresses, he was sitting crossed legged on them, completely naked. She tried not to stare, but her eyes seemed to have severed all communication with her brain.

"You have drawn nudes before, yes?"

She knew that if she tried to speak, her nervousness would be obvious, so she just nodded.

"Evie, is this going to be a problem? I mean, after the pond and all—"

"Yes, the pond. Well, see, that was the pond. Um, it was there. Not here. Not in my house."

"I just want to understand how you see me."

She took a calming breath, then nodded again.

"So how do you want me to pose?"

"Just make yourself comfortable. I work from your cues."

He tried leaning back on his hands, then uncrossing his legs, but finally came back to sitting crossing legged, his chin resting in his hand as he stared at her. Evie started drawing on the sketchpad, but almost immediately erased everything she had drawn. She tried again, only to rip the page from the sketchpad and crumple it up.

Finally, she moved to sit on the floor in front of him. She closed her eyes and focused on shutting out all thoughts from her mind. Then she opened her eyes again. This time, she didn't hesitate in her drawing. She drew the rough shape of his head first, then his shoulders and arms, working down the length of his body, focusing on the sculpt of his muscles. When she returned to his face, she sketched the relaxed curve of his mouth, the nose that was just a smidge too big to be perfectly proportioned for his face, and his well-defined cheekbones. Yet it was the tenderness in his eyes that she kept coming back to, tweaking her drawing until she could do no more.

When she finished, she sat back and looked at what she had done. The picture was a study of light and dark, strength and gentleness. It was the best sketch she'd ever drawn. She turned it around to show Jonathan.

"I've never seen anyone as beautiful as when you are drawing." He didn't even look at the sketch. "You bared your soul."

She felt a satisfied warmth flood her cheeks. "I've never bared my soul to anyone."

"You did to me, just now."

"Not knowingly." She whispered it, afraid it would upset him.

He cocked his head to the side. "Why don't you let people in?"

"Too hard." She shrugged and looked away.

He reached out to hold her chin, turning her face back to his. "It doesn't have to be." A faint smiled played across his lips. "I'm going to make love to you.

I don't care if the house falls down around us, nothing is going to stop me. This is your one chance to walk away."

She stared back at him, the power of his desire nearly knocking her over. When she was sure that her legs wouldn't collapse from under her, she stood and walked to the door. She closed it, then turned back to him.

"You live alone. You always close the door?"

She smiled. "Force of habit."

"Make new habits."

Her smile grew, and she opened door. Jonathan leaned back against the wall behind him, his face disappearing into the shadows. Evie moved to stand in front of him, then slowly removed her clothes, her heart beating faster as she dropped each article to the floor. When she finally stood before him, completely naked, she hesitated, unable to see his expression.

Jonathan leaned forward and took her hand, guiding her down to straddle his lap, never breaking eye contact with her. He explored her face with his fingers, as if he were drawing her features, tracing each eyebrow, her nose, and her cheeks. Finally, he rubbed his thumb along her jawline and then her lips. She'd never felt so beautiful.

"Jonathan, please." Evie saw the intensity spark in his eyes and for a moment she forgot how to breathe.

He gave her a half-smile. "Oh, Evie. I'm just beginning."

Chapter Eight

Jonathan propped his head on his hand and watched Evie sleeping. The early morning light filtered through the window, creating a hazy greyness that was caught between night and day. Jonathan could appreciate such a struggle, especially as he looked down at the woman curled into the blankets he'd hunted down in the middle of the night.

What was it about this woman? She was not what he would call drop-dead gorgeous. Her soft smile and defiant chin, even in sleep, were certainly pretty, but even just looking at her in the half-light, he felt his body reacting to her beyond any physical attraction. She wasn't afraid of anything, least of all exploration, which created an excitement in Jonathan that he'd never felt before.

Well, she was afraid of commitment, but that was fine with him. At twenty-three, he wasn't interested in a family any time soon. He brushed a lock of her dark hair back from her face, imagining how defiant she must have been as a child. She would certainly have rambunctious children, probably ten times as daring as she was. He chuckled. And ten times the handful.

She rolled on to her back and stretched, never opening her eyes. Her stomach growled, which made Jonathan chuckle even louder.

"Yeah, I'm hungry, too." He dipped his head to nibble on her ear.

She made a purring noise in the back of her throat. "I thought you were hungry."

"I am. For you."

It was almost noon when he finally let her get out of bed, although even then he couldn't stand not to be near her, touching her in some way. In the kitchen, she boiled some spaghetti and heated up tomato sauce. As she stood at the stove, stirring the sauce, Jonathan moved to the counter to stand next to her. He chopped up a head of lettuce for a salad, bumping his hip against hers every few seconds. Each bump was met with a giggle, then a bump in return.

By the time the meal was ready, Jonathan was no longer hungry—not for food at least. But Evie crossed her arms and gave him a look that told him to behave. He sat down at the small kitchen table and pretended to sulk.

"Oh, knock it off." She set a plate of spaghetti on the table before him, then ruffled his hair. "Eat. You're gonna need the energy."

He grabbed her hand and pulled her onto his lap, then instantly regretted it. He'd never be able to control himself with every inch of her within reach. He tried to focus on the food, swirling noodles around a fork and holding it up to her mouth. "You need your strength, too."

If he thought feeding her would cool his reaction to her proximity, he was sorely mistaken. Watching her eat the noodles off the fork was the most sensuous thing he'd ever seen. He swore loudly, then deposited her in the other chair. When she gave him a questioning look, he shook his head.

"You're trying my resolve, Evie. You have no idea."

"Right back at ya, Mr. Clark."

He knew she was trying to be playful, but he couldn't get past the thought the she was as excited as he was. It was an idea he had to put to the test.

He leaned over and licked the corner of her mouth. "You had some sauce."

"Uh-huh." Her response was thick with disbelief.

Jonathan moved to her chin. "And a bit here." He trailed kisses down her throat and across her collarbone.

"Okay, Mr. Clark. You win."

He moved up to her earlobe. "I win?"

She pushed him back slightly. "Don't make me say it again."

He stood and picked her up to carry her back upstairs. He almost made it, too.

"Wait, someone's here." She pointed out the front window. "Is that the same truck...?"

He let her feet drop so she could stand on her own. "Yeah. It's for me."

"Who knows you're here?"

Jonathan moved to the front door, hoping to catch his brother Daniel before he even got out of his truck, but just as he reached to open the front door, Daniel pounded on the other side.

"Jonathan Clark, get your ass out here now!"

Jonathan winced. "This isn't going to be pretty." He flashed an apologetic smile at Evie, then opened the door.

"Just what in the hell do you think you're doing, leaving me all alone to tend to them cattle?" Daniel's face reddened with each word.

"Sorry, man. Lost track of time."

Jonathan tried to step outside, but Daniel threw his arm up to block him, then pushed him to the side so he could see into the house. He nodded at Evie, then looked back at Jonathan. "What's the matter, horn dog, didn't get enough last week? Look, just save your play dates for when we're not in the middle of culling the herd."

Jonathan scowled at his brother. "Nice. Real classy."

Daniel shrugged as he walked back to his truck, then called over his shoulder, "Payback's a bitch."

When Jonathan turned back to apologize to Evie, she was already waving him out the door, laughing. "You'd better get going. Horn dog."

He wanted to stay, explain his brother's joking, explain that he hadn't had a girlfriend in almost a year. Actually, he wanted to stay and finish what they'd started in the kitchen. But if he didn't get back to the farm, he'd have to answer to Lucas. Bailing on Daniel was one thing. Bailing on Lucas—well, only really stupid people did that.

Jonathan gave Evie a quick peck on the cheek, then jogged out to his truck. Leaving now was not what he wanted, but it would be the smartest thing all around. As he drove out onto the country road, he told himself that a little space would be good, especially if Evie was the commitment-phobe she claimed to be. He didn't want to scare her away. Not now, not so soon. Not when he had so many other things in mind for her.

Chapter Nine

A week later, Evie had boxed up what was left of her great aunt's items and taken them to the auction house in Bender, finished painting the upstairs, set up her studio, and become completely bored. She hadn't heard from Jonathan, even though she'd half expected to see him over the weekend. The phone book she'd found in the kitchen was from 1984 and listed a handful of Clarks in the area. She'd found her way back to the steakhouse and had a burger, casually mentioning Jonathan in her conversation with the owner, but the woman didn't take the hint. Or didn't want to. So Evie returned home and decided to simply wait for him to show up again. When he was ready, he'd be back.

She just wished he'd hurry up and get ready.

The boredom of the country was driving her crazy. She told herself to make use of her studio, but every time she considered the idea, images of the night she spent with Jonathan plagued her, which only seemed to exacerbate her boredom. She was just too damned antsy to sit still.

She went out to the detached garage to poke around and see what she could find. She didn't expect much, so she was surprised to find a riding lawn mower that looked as if it had barely been used. After fiddling with the knobs and reading the sticker still attached to the seat, she figured out how to start it. Soon she was tearing through weeds and grass that had gone far too long without a nice buzz cut.

Unfortunately, her excitement about the mower was short lived. The passes back and forth across the lawn were even more monotonous than sitting and waiting for Jonathan to call. She decided to explore the twenty acres surrounding the house, using the lawn mower to cut a path behind the outbuildings, between the rows of mulberry trees, and out into ten acres that—according to the lawyer—could be rented out to the neighboring farmer for a nice little chunk of change. As soon as she had reached the far end of the property line, she turned the mower around to head back, at which point the machine sputtered and died. No amount of knob pulling or key turning would get it started again. She finally thought to check the gas tank. Empty.

It wouldn't have taken her long to walk back to the house if she could walk straight to it. Instead, she followed the path she'd cut, which was winding and exploratory. As she came up to the outbuildings, she heard a car door. She quickened her pace. Had Jonathan finally come back?

Soon she was running, afraid he'd find the house empty and leave without waiting for her to get back. When she rounded the corner of the house and the driveway came into view, she pulled up short.

"What the hell are you doing here?"

"Well I see why you want to stick around here for a bit longer." Liz held up the sketch of Jonathan. "Me likey the local farm boy."

·"Knock it off." Evie snatched the sketch from her sister and handed her a glass of iced tea instead, then joined her at the kitchen table.

"Well excuse me. But I think I have every right to be concerned when my baby sister quits her job through a text message. Really, a text message, Evie?"

Evie shrugged and sipped her tea. "Yes, you can be concerned, just like I can be concerned when my much older sister—"

"Watch it!"

Evie grinned. "When my sister shows up on my doorstep unannounced and with enough luggage to suggest an extended stay."

"Okay, I'll grant you that one. You can be concerned." She fidgeted with the glass of tea, spinning it back and forth on the table in front of her.

After several moments of silence, Evie couldn't stand it any longer. "So? What gives?"

Liz finally picked up her tea and took a sip, watching her sister over the rim of the glass. She set the glass back down and immediately started spinning it again.

Evie reached out to grab her sister's hand. "Jesus, Liz, what's wrong?"

"I'll tell you mine if you tell me about your farm boy. Deal?"

"Sure."

"Promise?"

Evie stuck out her tongue. "Yes, I promise."

"Hey, remember, I changed your diapers. I know all your tricks."

"Blah, blah, blah."

Liz folded her hands together on the table in front of her and stared at her iced tea for a moment, then looked up at Evie. "I left him."

Evie shook her head in confusion. "You left—"

And then understanding struck her, and she sucked in her breath. She watched her sister, afraid to react. She wanted to jump up and scream hallelujah, but she knew Liz would not appreciate such a reaction—no matter how well deserved.

"I think he's cheating on me." Liz kept her voice calm, even keeled, but Evie noted the tremble in her lip. "I decided that some time apart might do us some good."

Evie came around the table and put her arm around her sister's shoulders. "Oh, Liz, honey. I'm so sorry."

"It's just a trial separation—for now." Liz dropped her head to the table, her shoulders jerking in silent sobs.

Evie's skin went cold and her mouth was suddenly dry. "No, he loves you." The platitude sounded lame even to her.

Liz sat up and frowned at Evie. "I know he loves me. But when has love ever stopped a man from cheating?"

"Come on, Liz. You're not that woman."

"'That woman'—ha!" Liz wiped at her tears with a napkin. "I've become exactly that woman, thinking everything was all fine in my marriage while my husband was diddling his secretary." She rolled her eyes before Evie could say anything.

"Okay, yes, my marriage was not fine. But we were trying to have a baby—who does that if they're not committed to the marriage?"

Evie ran her hand along the edge of the table. "Well, Mom and Dad, for one."

Their family secret was no secret, especially as Liz was nearly ten years older than Evie. When they were younger, she'd told Evie all about the fights, the screaming from their parents' bedroom that had spilled out into the living room and then into the front yard for all the neighbors to see. Their father had cheated on their mother, and everyone knew. They'd stayed together, though, even trying to reconcile. One such reconciliation had resulted in Evie.

Now Liz was looking at Evie, a sour expression on her face. "Evelyn Jacobson! For once can you not make everything about you?"

Evie bit back the course retort she wanted to scream at her sister, and in the next second Liz was leaning over the table to hug Evie.

"Oh, I'm sorry! I didn't mean that—you know I didn't. I'm just all messed up."

Evie hugged her sister back. "I know, I know."

When Liz sat back down, she appeared to have calmed down, but that lasted for only a second or two. The tears started again. "Oh my God. Have I turned into Mom?"

"I dunno." Evie shrugged. "Are you cheating on your husband?"

The question silenced Liz, who stared at Evie, her mouth hanging open.

Evie made a mental note to let her mother know she'd spilled the beans—not that it would matter now, their parents having divorced soon after Evie's birth. But Liz would undoubtedly read their mother the riot act for not telling her first.

"Wait, what? No! You can't mean—how do you know?" Liz crossed her arms. "No, I don't believe it. I remember their arguments. I know I what I heard. Mom was always begging..." Her voice trailed off as she became lost in the memories.

Evie stood to refill their iced tea. She knew her sister was trying to sort through this new tidbit of information. When Evie sat back down at the table, Liz was shaking her head and smiling.

"I don't believe it. She kept that from me all these years." Her smile turned into laughter, and soon she was laughing so hard, new tears were running down her cheeks. "Any other family news I need to know about?" Before Evie could answer, Liz held up her hands. "No, never mind. Who wants to talk about such old news when we've got Mr. Hunk of the Month to talk about?" She held up the sketch of Jonathan.

Evie couldn't stop the flush that came to her cheeks when she saw the sketch and remembered how their night progressed.

"Evie! When did you start blushing about anyone?"

"Knock it off."

Liz smiled. "He must be something special. So when do I get to meet him?"

Evie groaned. "Whenever he decides to show up again."

"So call him, invite him to dinner."

"I don't know his phone number—and yes, I've tried to find it. I don't know anything about him except his name is Jonathan Clark, and he has a brother and works or lives on a farm." Now it was Evie's turn to fight back the tears, although hers were tears of frustration.

"Oh, a challenge!" Liz clapped in excitement. "Don't worry, we'll find your Mr. Clark. How hard could it be?"

Chapter Ten

Jonathan was kicking himself for not getting Evie's cell phone number when he had the chance.

In the past few weeks, he hadn't had a second to breathe, much less sneak over to see her. He and Daniel had gotten through culling the herd faster than in most years, which they chalked up to their brother Andrew still being in jail. Realizing how much more work they got done without Andrew's distractions, Daniel had become hell bent on getting a long list of chores done before Andrew returned, and he had been all too happy to enlist Jonathan in the work.

When Jonathan balked, Daniel said, "Payback's a bitch."

"Yeah, you already got me back, remember?"

Daniel shrugged. "Let's just say I'm banking this against future needs."

"I'm sure you could use some time off to go see Alex."

Daniel's frown would have been terrifying to most people. "I won't be seeing Alex for a while. Seems someone told her dad about our secret meetings."

Jonathan doubled over in laughter.

"Yeah, I thought I had you to thank for that one."

"Whoa, it wasn't me—swear!"

But Daniel didn't believe him and decided that, as long as he was miserable not being able to see Alex, Jonathan would be miserable right alongside him. And Daniel watched him like a hawk to ensure that he did not get a single moment of reprieve.

Jonathan considered going to Lucas for help, but the eldest Clark was actually almost smiling lately, and Jonathan refused to be responsible for anything that would interfere with even a glimpse of happiness for the man. He'd come back from the war in Afghanistan a widower with a newborn daughter. It had been nearly ten years since his return, and this was the first time that Jonathan saw hints of the old Lucas. He no longer had the tightness around his mouth or the hardness in his eyes. If Jonathan went to Lucas about Daniel's slave-driving and the hardness returned, Jonathan would never forgive himself. None of the Clarks would forgive him.

When he couldn't stand it any longer, Jonathan finally decided to take matters into his own hands. He waited until everyone was asleep, then crept out of the house.

It was nearly 3 a.m. when he put his truck in neutral and pushed it down the lane—something he never wanted to have to do again. Twenty minutes later, sweaty and out of breath, he was out on the road. He started the truck, saying a silent prayer that it wouldn't wake his brothers, then put the thought from his mind. He'd deal with them when he got back, after a few hours of Evie's kisses.

Not even five minutes later, he was standing on the edge of the country road, cursing at the flat tire and at the mysterious disappearance of his spare. His shouting intensified when he found the thick bolt stuck in the sidewall of the tire. He was going to throttle Daniel.

By the time he walked back to their farm, the horizon was already lightening, which made it easy for him to spot his sister in the lane, returning from her own night spent away.

Susannah stood watching him, her arms crossed. "Do I even want to know?"

Jonathan smiled. "Only if you want to share your own."

She blanched in the early morning light.

"Jeez, Suz, is it that bad?"

"What? No." Her forced laughed didn't fool him for a second.

He stepped closer, frowning. "Fess up. Who is it?"

"Fine, but if I tell you, you can't say a word to anyone until I figure everything out."

"Okay."

"Promise."

He held up both hands. "I promise, I promise."

She scowled, shifting back and forth before saying, "Tate Trudell."

Jonathan felt like he'd been hit by a truck.

"Oh, no, Jonathan. Please tell me it's not that bad."

He shook his head. "Are you trying to kill Lucas? Is that what this is all about? Finally send him around the bend?"

She was shaking her head. "What are you talking about?"

Jonathan wondered how much of the history he should share with his sister. Then he remembered how worried he'd been about upsetting Lucas now that he was just starting to return to his old self. Susannah had a right to know about their brother's wife, Mary Ellen, especially as Susannah's path could lead her on a collision course with the bad blood between Lucas and his former best friend.

He took Susannah by the arm and led her to the porch, easing her down onto the front steps. "Look, I don't know the specifics, but I do know that the reason Tate left all those years ago was because Mary Ellen had feelings for him. Him leaving suggests that he didn't feel the same about her, if that's what you're worried about."

"No—no, that's not it." She grabbed Jonathan's arm tightly. "He said he'd get Lucas' approval. I made him promise, but he said he'd take care of it."

Jonathan let out a low whistle. "Well, you know what that means?"

"What?"

"That Tate Trudell is in love with you." Jonathan frowned at his sister. "And by that bright rosy color in your cheeks, I take it that you love him too. Oh, baby sis, I wouldn't want to be you right about now." He put his arm around her shoulder, and she leaned into him.

"It'll be all right. Tell me it'll all work out."

"It'll work out, Suz. It has to."

"You don't sound very convinced."

He didn't feel very convinced. He was more concerned about Lucas and his nine-year-old daughter, Jenny. She wouldn't remember the intensity of her father's anger when he'd first returned from the war and had been forced to face the reality of his life on the farm, but it was a fury that had terrified them all. How would Jenny react if she saw that in her father now? And Jonathan had no doubts that Lucas finding out that his little sister was in love with his former best friend would send him right back into that pit of anger.

Jonathan reassured Susannah, then headed off to find Daniel, hoping his brother would not be too distracted by Alex to help keep an eye on events as they unfolded with Lucas. Jonathan frowned. He wasn't going to get to see Evie for a while yet. He hoped she'd forgive him for the long absence— although she did say she didn't like commitments. He'd just have to convince her that he was giving her space. If she ever spoke to him again.

He might just have to throttle Daniel anyway.

Chapter Eleven

Evie tried to put thoughts about Jonathan out of her mind. It wasn't hard to do during the day. She and Liz fell into an easy routine: Evie would spend the early morning hours working in her studio while Liz researched options for decorating the house. Interior design was her sister's forte, but she'd given it up when she decided to get pregnant.

Evie could tell how much Liz missed her design business, as every afternoon her sister would drag her across several counties, exploring shops that advertised "antiques" but were mostly just used goods. No matter how small the store or how worthless the "antiques," Liz would not be deterred, and she inevitably found something that made her chatter with excitement, especially when she learned just how little the owner was asking for the piece.

Evie knew the treasure hunt was helping her sister keep her mind off her own troubles, so she couldn't complain. Plus, Evie did come home exhausted nearly every evening, which helped her sleep through the nights.

Most nights.

Some nights the thoughts of Jonathan would peck at her brain, refusing to let her sleep no matter how exhausted her body was. Why had he not stopped by to see her? And why couldn't she and Liz seem to find him? They had asked around in Bender at the city offices and the local coffee shop, but any information they might have gotten either sent them on a wild goose chase or was simply flat out wrong. Evie's frustration was turning into anger as she wondered if Jonathan Clark was even his real name.

Occasionally, she would hear her sister's muffled crying through the wall at night, which made her feel guilty about worrying about Jonathan. She and Jonathan were at best a one-night fling at this point. Her sister was mourning her marriage of almost a decade.

After one particularly difficult night, during which Evie tossed and turned, desperate to forget the night she and Jonathan spent together, she finally got up to brew some coffee only to find Liz already making breakfast, a huge grin on her face.

"How can you be so chipper when the sun's barely up?"

Liz set a plate with eggs, bacon, hash browns, and waffles on the table in front of Evie.

"Jeez, have you been cooking all night?" Evie shoved the plate away. "I just need coffee. Black, black coffee."

Liz poured her a mug of coffee, then dropped a newspaper on the table. "I think I figured out a solution to your farm boy problem." She pointed to an ad for a street dance in the neighboring town.

"No, forget about it." Evie sipped at the coffee, pretending she could feel the caffeine surging through her body and fortifying her against the memories of Jonathan.

"What do you mean, 'forget about it'? Do I need to pull the sketch out and remind you of his hunkiness?"

"No! I definitely don't need reminding of him— of anything."

Liz sat down across from Evie, a knowing look on her face. She picked at the plate of food, breaking off a piece of waffle and popping it in her mouth.

Evie just shook her head. "Seriously, this chipperness? I'm gonna think you're on drugs or something."

Liz shrugged.

"Come on. Spill it."

Liz clasped her hands together and sat up straight, as if preparing for a job interview. "So you know the pieces I've been buying on our little jaunts?"

"Of course. They've taken over the living room."

Liz waved away her comment. "Yes, yes. I sent some pics of them to a design contact in Denver." She rubbed her hands together.

"And?"

"Remember that mirror I found?"

She didn't, but she wasn't about to tell her sister that. "Sure."

"My contact offered me $200 plus postage to send it to her." When Evie just smiled, Liz got up and went to the living room, retuning with a mirror a bit larger than a manila folder. Its thick wooden edges had intricate carvings of various flowers.

"Wait, $200 for that? Didn't you pay like—"

"Less than $40, yes."

"Nice score." Evie took several long drinks on her rapidly cooling coffee.

"It got me thinking, so I sent out information to a few other contacts."

"And?"

"And now you need to hurry and get dressed so we can get all the packages to the post office."

Evie pouted when Liz cleared off the table, including the coffee mug that was still nearly full. "Can't we just have a day to relax and do nothing?"

"Sure we can." Liz folded her arms across her chest. "A nice, long day of rest, relaxation, and thoughts about your farm boy."

Evie stuck her tongue out at her sister before heading to get dressed.

An hour later, Evie left Liz at the Harrington post office, where she was discussing insurance with the employee, and walked across the street to the town's coffee shop, which was really just a gas station that sold incredibly strong coffee and offered a place to sit while customers attempted to drink it. She was happy that Liz was able to funnel her energy into her antiquing project, and she had to admit that the thought of her sister staying with her indefinitely was a huge relief. Evie didn't think she could handle a quiet house.

Although she wasn't too happy about her sister dictating what to wear in public. Liz had nixed Evie's jeans and t-shirt, instead handing her a simple peach sun dress that fell to just above the knees. When Evie balked, Liz launched into a spiel about how it was important to look nice in public as they never knew who they might run into. Evie put on the dress just to get Liz to shut up.

Now, as Evie entered the gas station, she felt the chill of air-conditioning and rubbed her hands together. "Would serve her right if I got sick from wearing this thing."

She smiled at the three elderly ladies who sat in one of the booths as she walked to the wall with the coffee pot. She poured herself a large cup of coffee, then stood at the counter, waiting to pay the clerk, an older man who was engrossed in the newspaper.

Evie cleared her throat. "Excuse me." She waved a twenty-dollar bill in the air, but the man didn't look up.

"Won't do any good." The familiar voice in her ear and warm breath on her neck caused goose bumps all along Evie's arms. "Larry's deaf as a doornail."

She spun around to confront Jonathan, but he was already grabbing her hand and pulling her down a small hallway.

"Wait, my coffee—"

She tried to reach back for the steaming cup, frustrated that no one was letting her enjoy a simple cup of coffee, but Jonathan didn't slow down. He opened the door to a unisex bathroom and pulled her inside, closing the door behind them before pinning her to the door with a deep, urgent kiss that left her knees shaky.

When he finally pulled back, she slumped into him. "Screw the coffee. Give me more of that."

Jonathan chuckled as he dotted kisses along the side of her neck. "God, I've missed you."

"Yeah, speaking of that." She pushed back on his shoulders, trying to put space between them.

"Evie."

"Don't you give me that sexy little growl, Jonathan. Where the hell have you been? You think you can just take off and that'd be it? Not stop by? Send carrier pigeons? Smoke signals? Something? I don't know what kind of girls you're used to, but I don't do the whole one-night stand thing. And why the hell are you smiling?"

"You think I'm sexy."

"I said growl—your growl is sexy."

He made a growling noise in the back of his throat.

"Oh, knock it off. I want answers—"

He cut off her protests with another kiss, this one just as urgent, but instead of feeling rushed, it was slow, explorative, possessing—and it made Evie forget all about her objections as her body screamed for more, reminding her how badly she'd missed him. She felt like an addict who was finally getting a rush from her drug of choice, only this drug was more gratifying than anything she'd ever experienced.

She returned his kisses, clinging to him, her fingernails digging into his back. The more she fed her addiction, the more demanding it became. She didn't care. She matched Jonathan's intensity and then some. When his knee parted her legs, she wrapped herself around it. When his hand slid under her dress, her entire body was on fire—a fire she was desperate to be consumed by.

Without stopping the kiss, Jonathan dropped his other hand to slide under her dress as well. He lifted his knee just enough that Evie had to cling to his neck as she was raised a few inches off the ground. He hooked his fingers on her panties, then pulled, dropping his knee at the same time.

Evie fell back against the door, trying to catch her breath as Jonathan bent down and pulled her panties completely off. When he stood up again, he put one hand on the door and held up the panties in the other hand, a playful smile on his lips.

"Did you forget our agreement?"

Evie grabbed at the waistband to his jeans, pulling him to her. "Save the lecture."

The playful smile disappeared, and in that instant, she saw understanding flicker across his face, only to be immediately replaced with a desire that matched her own. He licked his bottom lip, and Evie reached out to pull his lips to hers, the intense kiss turning voracious.

A knock sounded on the door, but they ignored it, their need too great to stop.

"Jonathan?" The female voice from the other side of the door was hushed, but urgent.

Evie started to pull away, but Jonathan grabbed the back of her head to hold her in place.

"Jonathan Clark. Don't make me come in there and get you."

Jonathan growled again, but this time in frustration instead of desire. Finally, he broke off the kiss and pushed a shaky Evie away from the door. "I'll be keeping these." He shoved the panties into his jeans pocket, then was gone, slamming the door behind him.

It took Evie several deep breaths to calm her body down enough to be able to think, but then her thoughts started racing and her blood was once again burning, albeit for a different reason. "What the hell?" She threw open the door and stepped out into the hall, yelling, "What the hell!"

Jonathan was nowhere to be seen. A tall brunette standing by the counter, her skin a perfect golden brown, turned to look at Evie. She shook her head slightly.

"Where'd he go?" Evie stormed up to the counter, clenching her fists. "Was that you knocking on the door? What's going on? Where'd he go?"

The woman took a step back from Evie. "He didn't say anything about seeing you."

Evie pressed her fingers to her temples and tried to take a calming breath. It didn't work. "What the hell? Just tell me what is going on!"

The bell above the gas station's door rang, and the brunette glanced over, her eyes growing wide. She grabbed Evie's arm and pulled her close enough to be heard as she hissed, "Don't say anything!" Then she let go, pushing Evie away to look at the newcomer, a huge smile spreading across her face. "Daddy!"

"Where is he? Where is that son of a bitch?"

The brunette's father was a round, balding man whose loss of hair was even more evident as the skin on his forehead was now a deep, mottled red.

The brunette rushed to his side to hold his hand, patting it repeatedly. "Daddy, calm down. There's no one here but us girls—well, and Larry."

"Bullshit!"

"Language, Mr. Porter."

Everyone turned to the trio of elderly ladies sitting in the booth. The one who spoke was smiling sweetly at the man. The second was beaming at the brunette. The third was staring at Evie, a knowing smile on her lips. Evie got the distinct feeling that the woman staring at her knew what she'd been doing in the bathroom with Jonathan. She tried to keep her cheeks from burning bright red, but the more she tried, the hotter her cheeks felt. Another glance at the woman and Evie could tell she was having a hard time controlling her laughter.

"You'll have to excuse my language, Sisters Carter. We're talking about that damn Clark boy, who won't keep his hands off my daughter."

Evie's attention snapped back to the balding man, who was glaring at Larry behind the counter.

"Where is he? I saw him come in here!"

Larry shook his head and shrugged, dropping the newspaper on the counter.

"You!" Mr. Porter focused on Evie, pointing at her. "Who are you? Oh, never mind. Tell me, did you see a boy come in her—tall, brown hair?"

Evie opened her mouth to answer, but nothing came out. She licked her lips and tried swallowing several times, but it didn't help. She tried to keep her eyes on the balding man, but she kept looking at the brunette, unable to stop an image of her and Jonathan together from forming in her head. The harder she tried to push it away, the more detailed it became.

"Goodness, Mr. Porter. You've scared the poor thing." The Carter sister who'd already warned Mr. Porter about his language was now looking at Evie.

The third sister shook her head. "Oh, I don't think anything scares this one."

The brunette frowned at the sisters, then hurried over to stand by Evie, linking arms with her. "Now, Daddy, you be polite. This is Miss Evie Jacobson—you know, Lillian Walters' family? She's staying in Mrs. Walters' home, taking care of it. We were just getting to know each other when you interrupted us."

She frowned at her father once again when he opened his mouth to speak. He snapped it shut and crossed his arms. The brunette slid her arm from Evie's, then grasped her hand, turning so her father couldn't see her face.

"Well, Evie, like I was saying before my father decided to cause such a scene, my name is Alexandria Porter, but you can call me Alex. Everyone does." She nodded at Evie, encouraging her to play along.

Evie glance from Alex to her father and back again. "Nice to meet you." Her voice was quiet, unconvincing. How could she convince them of anything when she couldn't believe it herself. Why was she playing along with this charade, holding hands with Jonathan's—what, toy? Conquest? Girlfriend? And how did she know so much about Evie? Had Jonathan shared such information during their pillow talk? Laughing about the newcomer he had eating out of his hand?

Evie realized they were all still waiting for her to speak, and she had to fight the urge to scream at them all. "Porter. As in Porterhouse Bar?"

"Now see there, Daddy?" Alex flashed a smile at her father. "You're trying to scare a customer."

"I'm gonna do a whole lot more if I find out that Clark boy is in here and—"

The bell above the door rang again, and everyone turned to see a man, his white hair cut in a close crew cut, stick his head in the door. "Hey, Porter, we got the Clark boy's truck out here."

Mr. Porter rushed outside, followed by Alex and then Evie, who was determined to get some answers. Just as they walked outside, she saw Jonathan's truck speed by and head to the end of the block.

"See, Daddy? I told you he wasn't in the gas station."

Mr. Porter harrumphed loudly before moving down the street in the opposite direction. Evie and Alex watched him go, then Alex turned to Jonathan's truck, which had stopped at the corner, its turn signal flashing. Alex blew a quick kiss at the truck, which was met with the brake lights flashing twice before the truck turned and sped off.

"Thank you." Alex grabbed Evie's hand and squeezed it. "I owe you a big one. See you at the dance tonight? Everyone will be there." She didn't wait for an answer as she rushed to catch up with her father, leaving Evie standing on the sidewalk, trying to figure out everything that just happened.

She was still standing there when Liz crossed the street. "Hey, you ready to head back home?"

Evie shook her head. "I have absolutely no idea."

"Did you get your coffee?"

"Nope."

"Okay." Liz cocked her head to the side. "Everything all right?"

Evie finally looked at her sister. "No. And you know why? Because you made me wear this stupid dress." She spun around and took several steps toward the car, then stopped and looked back at her sister. "Well come on. Hurry up. I gotta get ready for this dance tonight."

Liz jogged to catch up with her. "Oh, so we're going now?" She clapped her hands. "Think we'll see the farm boy?"

"Oh, we'll see him, but I don't think anyone will be too happy about it—least of all him."

Chapter Twelve

The last place Jonathan wanted to be at that moment was the street dance. Ever since being dragged away from Evie that morning, he'd been in a foul mood, which was further exacerbated by his brother Daniel and his antagonism. But he and Daniel had finally come to an agreement: They would both put their other siblings, Lucas and Susannah, ahead of their own one-upmanship for the time being—especially with Andrew being released from jail today. In other words, Daniel would stop blaming Jonathan for telling Alex's father about them, and Jonathan would wait to throttle his older brother for putting him in the middle and preventing him from seeing Evie.

Daniel and Jonathan hatched a plan to get Lucas to go to the street dance. It was a long shot, as their brother had avoided most public functions since returning from the war in Afghanistan, but both brothers were determined to try. Daniel saw it as an opportunity to spend some time with Alex, as no one questioned Lucas, not even Mr. Porter. Jonathan, on the other hand, knew that Susannah would have a better chance of bringing Lucas and Tate back together in a public place as neither man would cause a scene when others were watching. And, if everything went well—a big if, Jonathan realized—he might find a few moments to slip over to Evie's and finally spend some more time with her.

He'd missed Evie terribly the last few weeks. He had told himself he just needed a little more time with her, time to explore her body and get his fill. Then the novelty would wear off, and he wouldn't have such a hard time getting her out of his thoughts. But today's run-in proved that he'd been fooling himself. He didn't just crave a little more physical satisfaction. Her spontaneity, her willingness to share her passion with him openly, and her lack of fear in knowing what she wanted and going after it excited him beyond any physical response. During the drive home, he'd wondered if he'd ever get tired of her brazenness. Somehow, he didn't think he would.

When he and Daniel entered the house, they were shocked to find Lucas sitting in the living room, dressed in his nice jeans and a pressed shirt. Lucas leveled at stare at them that dared them to make any sort of comment on his attire. Neither brother said a word.

Their niece Jenny entered the living room with an overdramatic waving of her arms and rolling of her eyes that made Jonathan smile—although he hid it so Jenny wouldn't see. "There you are! I've been looking for you all day."

Being on Lucas' bad side would be bad enough. Causing his nine-year-old niece any measure of discomfort would result in the whole family turning on him—not that he could ever knowingly hurt Jenny, who'd already had to deal with growing up without her mother and a father who never spoke. Well, not to anyone but her. Jonathan frowned as he glanced at Lucas. It was the one area where he didn't respect his older brother: letting his own personal demons leak out and affect his daughter. Jenny had been forced to grow up far too quickly. Looking at Lucas, he realized that his brother was fully aware that his shortcomings had impacted his daughter. Even though he beamed with pride when he looked at Jenny, Lucas had a dullness in his eyes that hadn't been there before Afghanistan, a sort of disconnect with the world. Jonathan gritted his teeth, his frown deepening, but this time the disgust was turned on himself. Who was he to pass judgment on Lucas, a man who spent eighteen months on the front lines of the war?

Daniel hugged Jenny's shoulders, pulling her close to him. "You know, there's this new invention called a phone. Maybe you've heard of it?"

Jenny rolled her eyes. "Like I didn't try that. I guess no one bothers to answer their phones anymore."

Lucas crossed his arms and glared first at Daniel, then at Jonathan.

"Well, we're here now," Jonathan said, ignoring Lucas as best he could. "So what's up?"

"I have an announcement to make." She pulled away from Daniel and walked into the center of the room, her chin thrust out just enough that she had to look down her nose to see. "A very big announcement."

"I see that I'm right on time, then."

Everyone turned to see Andrew standing in the doorway. Jenny ran to hug her uncle, then pulled him back to the center of the room, barely letting him shake Daniel's hand as he passed. He reached out to shake Jonathan's hand.

"Glad you're back, Andrew."

"I would've been home sooner if I could've gotten the same deal as you and Danny boy." Andrew's grip tightened and he pulled Jonathan closer. "We got lots to talk about, don't we, little brother?"

Jonathan nodded almost imperceptibly toward Lucas, whose black stare was drilling into Andrew. Andrew dropped Jonathan's hand and spun around to face Jenny.

"Now, what about this announcement?"

With all eyes focused on her, Jenny suddenly blushed and looked at the floor. "I was kinda hoping to share it when Aunt Suz got back, but there's no time now." She looked up at Lucas, unable to control the smile spreading across her face, and clasped her hands together. "Daddy's agreed to take me out on a date. With him. First an early dinner at the Porterhouse, and then dancing at the street dance."

The three younger brothers turned to look at Lucas, whose smile was almost as big as Jenny's.

"Well, alrighty then!" Andrew grabbed Jonathan, flinging an arm around his shoulders. "Looks like we're gonna have one heckuva celebration at the dance tonight. Guess I'd better go get ready myself." He stopped as he passed Jenny and bowed deeply in front of her. "I hope you'll save at least one dance for your old uncle?"

Jenny giggled and nodded, and then Andrew headed upstairs. Lucas stood and held out his arm to Jenny, who wrapped both of her hands around it, then followed as her father escorted her out. Once the door slammed behind them, Jonathan and Daniel exchanged an uneasy look. They both knew what would happen if Andrew discovered either brother's interest in a member of the fairer sex, and neither wanted to have to deal with his taunts all evening—or subject others to them.

In addition to keeping Andrew in the dark, Jonathan would have to keep an eye on Lucas, who would likely encounter Sheriff Tate Trudell at the dance. Jonathan didn't know if Susannah had managed to talk to Tate yet and figure out what to do. He would have to stick by Lucas, no matter what. He didn't want Lucas to be sent away for murdering the sheriff on the same day that Andrew was released.

Jonathan was losing all hope that he would be able to slip away and find Evie, but his disappointment was balanced by the fact that Lucas was going to a public function. A fun public function. Jonathan couldn't remember the last time he'd done that.

After half an hour of watching couples dance, Jonathan was desperate to go find Evie. Unfortunately, his family didn't seem to be all that accommodating of his secret desire to leave. He and Daniel were sitting at a picnic table, staring at Lucas' back as their older brother watched the people dancing. Andrew stood a few feet away, making catcalls at the younger girls on the dance floor. Jonathan was disgusted by Andrew and convinced that Lucas was watching one particular platinum blond on the dance floor. Neither Susannah nor Sheriff Trudell had made an appearance yet, and Jonathan bristled at the thought that they might be hidden away together somewhere, avoiding public scrutiny. Jonathan wanted his sister to be happy, but dang it, he wanted to be happy too, and sitting here babysitting his brothers was not making him happy at all.

He was just about to offer up some excuse so he could leave when he saw Jenny leading Susannah toward the picnic table. Susannah sat next to Lucas and leaned in to talk to him. Lucas nodded, but made no other indication that he was listening. Jonathan wished he could hear what his sister was saying. If she was telling Lucas about Tate, there might still be time to sneak over to Evie's tonight, but he couldn't imagine Lucas reacting so calmly to news that his little sister was in love with the same man Lucas' wife claimed to have loved.

Jenny pulled Susannah away from her father. "Aunt Suz, the funnel cake guy's here. C'mon."

Susannah looked at Lucas. "When I get back, okay?" She threw Jonathan a look begging for help, but he shrugged, not sure what he was supposed to do. What had she told Lucas? Anything? Everything? He wasn't about to broach the subject with Lucas until he knew what Susannah had said.

A few minutes later, when he saw Tate walking straight toward Lucas, Jonathan nudged Daniel. "We best make ourselves scarce."

Daniel started to protest, then saw Tate and blanched. He couldn't move fast enough to get away from the impending confrontation.

Jonathan motioned for Andrew to follow, but the older Clark spat on the ground to show his disgust. Jonathan didn't know if Andrew was more upset with them giving Lucas and Tate room to talk or with the sheriff in general. He wasn't about to stick around and find out. If Andrew's temper got him landed back in jail again, Jonathan wanted to be as far from the scene as possible.

He caught up with Daniel just as his brother saw Alex on the other side of the dance floor. Daniel moved to stand next to a crowd of people, hiding his face as he looked around for Alex's father.

"Good God, Daniel. Grow a pair already."

Daniel snarled at him, then squared his shoulders and made his way through the dancers, a man on a mission. However, when the other couples parted and scattered applause erupted around him, Daniel spun around, his fear of being caught plastered across his face. Jonathan burst out laughing as he realized the applause was for a new couple on the dance floor. He moved to Daniel's elbow and dragged him over to Alex. He was going to have to get these two together soon if he hoped to find Evie tonight.

He wished he had thought to tell her to come to the dance tonight. It would have made everything so much easier, especially now that Andrew was distracted by Tate and Lucas. Then again, she had done her own fair share of distracting when he ran into her. He couldn't help smiling at the memory.

"I know that look, Johnny." Alex was practically giggling as she patted his chest. "You're in love."

"So you've finally caught on." He grabbed her hand and held it in both of his, lifting it to brush a quick kiss across her knuckles. "And here I thought I'd have to fight my own brother to win your heart."

She laughed outright at his exaggerated acting.

Meanwhile, Daniel looked as if he were ready to bash his brother's head in. "You're not funny, you know."

Jonathan shrugged and blew a kiss toward Alex.

Suddenly Daniel's anger vanished, replaced by a smugness that made Jonathan wary. "And clearly I'm not the only one who doesn't appreciate your humor." He nodded at someone behind Jonathan.

When Jonathan turned to look, the laughter died from his lips. Evie and Liz stood just behind him, both staring in his direction. Evie was chewing on her bottom lip as her glance slid from him to Alex and then back again. The betrayal he saw in her eyes felt like he'd been sucker punched. He opened his mouth to explain, but he couldn't breathe, and no words would come out.

Suddenly, a crack echoed above the noise around them. A hushed silence fell, with the musicians taking notice as they stopped playing, as if on cue.

"Don't you ever speak to me like that, Andrew Clark!"

Jonathan whipped around to see Andrew raising his hand toward Susannah. A cold fury rose inside him. He didn't know what was happening between his brother and sister, but if Andrew touched Susannah, he'd be sorely beaten before the police could intervene. Daniel must have had the same idea because he took a step toward the confrontation, his hands clenched in fists.

But Susannah wasn't backing down either. "So that's how it's gonna be? Then take your best shot." She turned her face slightly, giving him full access to her cheek. Jonathan sucked in a hissing breath, preparing himself to launch at his older brother.

Instead of striking her, Andrew howled in pain. Lucas stood behind him, holding his arm back.

"You strike her, brother, and I'll kill you myself." Lucas' quiet voice rang out above the crowd, and

Jonathan instantly went from wanting to harm Andrew to being afraid for his brother's life. Lucas jerked on Andrew's arm again. "Momma would be ashamed of you, hearing you speak like that to your own sister." After another moment, he let Andrew shrug his arm out of the hold. "We're not going to have a problem here, are we?"

"A problem? A problem!" Andrew was sputtering in rage. "What, and I suppose you're fine with our sister giving away the goods to Tate?"

"Yes, I am."

Jonathan realized he'd been holding his breath and suddenly let it go in a burst of relief. Lucas knew, and he was okay with Tate and Susannah. And he was speaking again! Jonathan wanted to shout out in excitement. He spun around to grab Evie and hold on to her until he could explain that he'd been joking with Alex, but his excitement evaporated when she was nowhere to be found. In her place, he saw Jenny, who was watching the scene between her father and uncle. He also saw the look of panic cross her face when Andrew spoke again.

"Really? After what he did with Mary Ellen?" Andrew spit on the ground at Lucas' feet. "You disgust me."

Jonathan moved to put his arm around Jenny and take her away from the mess Andrew was creating, but she stepped past him.

"What did he do to my mother?" She stood at the edge of the crowd, staring at her father. "Daddy? What did he do to my mother?"

"Nothing, sweetheart, he didn't do anything. Your Uncle Andrew is just confused, that's all." Lucas flashed a glare toward Andrew, daring him to contradict him, then held out his hand to Jenny, who took it. "Tate Trudell is my best friend, but we lost touch for a while. Now, thanks to your aunt, we're gonna be friends again. That's all."

"And my mother?"

He leaned down to whisper to her, then leaned back and winked at her. "Hey, weren't you supposed to bring me a funnel cake?"

Jenny groaned and rolled her eyes in an exaggerated manner. "The line was so long!"

The crowd started whispering all around Jonathan, the townspeople finally reacting now that they knew there would be no bloodshed. He was sure the rumor mills would be flying over coffee the next morning. But he didn't care. Let them gossip. Lucas was back and was clearly okay with Susannah being in love with Tate. Now he just had to find Evie and explain the situation to her. She'd laugh when he told her it was all a joke. Wouldn't she?

He scanned the crowd, but he saw no sign of Evie or her sister.

"They left."

He glanced at Daniel, who was holding Alex tightly around the waist. "What?"

"They left. When Susannah slapped Andrew. Man, she walloped him good. I didn't think she'd survived there for a minute, but can you believe Lucas? I almost forgot what his voice sounded like."

Jonathan held up both hands. "Enough! What do you mean they left?"

Daniel snorted in reply.

"Go after her." Alex pulled away from Daniel and stood on her tiptoes to whisper into Jonathan's ear. "She's in love, too."

Chapter Thirteen

Evie whipped around yet another car and jammed her foot against the accelerator, pushing past the car in front of them before swerving back into the correct lane. She should have let Liz drive home. To Liz's credit, she didn't say a word about Evie's erratic driving, although she repeatedly held out her hands toward the dash, as if warding off an impending crash.

Evie missed the turn to her great aunt's house and swore, using a string of profanities that left her gasping for breath.

"If we make it home alive, you're going to have to teach me what half those words mean."

Evie glanced at her sister, scowling so tightly she'd lost feeling in her lips. But when she saw how tightly

Liz was clutching the grab-handle above the window with one hand while steadying herself with her other hand, Evie couldn't help but laugh.

The laughter almost immediately turned to sobs that wracked her entire body and left her gasping for breath. She lifted her foot from the accelerator and the car slowed to a crawl on the highway, causing angry horns to blare at them.

"Jesus, Evie, get off the road!" Liz reached over to crank the steering wheel toward her, and the car drifted into the ditch, jerking to a halt when the front bumper crashed into the far side of the ditch.

Both looked around at the darkness surrounding them, then looked back at each other. A second later, they erupted into a cathartic laughter, and Evie felt her acrimony drain away. Several minutes later, she and Liz were both wiping at the tears streaming down their faces.

"Oh, we are quite the pair, Evelyn Jacobson."

"That we are, Elizabeth Jacobson Miller."

Liz groaned. "Do we have neon signs on our foreheads that say 'Losers welcome'?"

"No, it's not us. It's them." Evie crossed her arms over the top of the steering wheel and rested her chin on her arms. "Losers are looking for some way to improve their lot in life, so naturally they're attracted to us."

They were silent for a moment, watching the headlights from the passing cars wash across the soybean field spread out before them. A few cars slowed, as if to offer help, but Evie stuck her hand out the window and waved them on.

"How do you do that?"

Evie looked at Liz from the corner of her eye. "Do what?"

"Not blame yourself."

Evie shrugged. "If I blamed myself, I'd be a doormat, like—" She bit back her words as she turned to her sister.

"Like me. You can say it. It's nothing I haven't thought before."

"No, I didn't mean it like that." Evie reached out for her sister's hand, but Liz jerked away, turning to look out her window.

"At least I don't run away from everything."

Evie bristled at the comment, but she didn't respond, no matter how badly she wanted to point out that Liz had done just that when she came to Nebraska. She couldn't say that, though, because leaving her husband had—in Evie's opinion—been the best thing Liz could have done.

Sighing, Evie put the car in reverse and backed out of the ditch, then maneuvered them back onto the highway, heading back toward the correct turnoff.

Running away had always worked well for her. It wasn't that she was avoiding her problems, but more that she wanted to evaluate the situation. If staying would not benefit her, she would choose to move on. Liz, however, was of the belief that she needed to stay and face her problems if she wanted to grow as a person. Evie frowned. If growing as a person meant marrying a man who didn't love her, she'd prefer to just keep running.

Neither sister spoke as they drove along the gravel road that led to the house. Evie wasn't sure how to bring Liz out of her own dark thoughts, but she really wanted to talk to her about Jonathan and what they'd seen at the dance. The closer they got to the house, the more annoyed she became. Liz had had weeks to adjust to the realization that her husband was cheating on her. Evie had just found out about Jonathan today. Her older sister should be consoling her, but instead she was pouting because Evie—in a state of emotional distress—had inadvertently called her sister a doormat.

"Truth hurts," Evie mumbled to herself as they turned down the lane to the house.

Liz lurched forward. "Oh, shit!"

At the end of the lane was a dark sedan. Evie frowned, not recognizing the car. She was about to ask Liz about it, when she saw her brother-in-law sitting on the front steps leading to the house.

"Oh, shit is right!"

"No, no, no." Liz shook her head. "I'm not dealing with this. Not now, not yet."

Evie rolled her eyes, fighting the instinct to point out that Liz was, in fact, running away yet again. "You're going to have to deal with it sooner or later."

"No, not now. Just leave." Liz reached over, as if to steer the car from the passenger seat, but Evie slapped her hands away.

"I'm not leaving my own house. I've had a really crappy day, and I just want to go to bed and forget about everything. If you don't want to deal with him, then tell him to leave."

"Okay, yes. Leave. I'll tell him to leave."

Evie pulled the car to a stop and turned off the engine, but before she could open her door, Liz was clutching at her arm.

"I can't do it. I'm too weak. You tell him to leave. Please, Evie."

Evie started to protest, but Liz pulled her into a quick embrace, then shot out the passenger-side door and raced up the walk, pushing past her husband. A wave of nausea overcame Evie when she noted that the man on the steps didn't even try to stop Liz.

"Of course not. He's staring at me." She clenched her fists in an attempt to prepare for the inevitable confrontation, then slid out of the car, slamming the door behind her. "Asshole." By the time she walked around the back of the car, he was already at the end of the walkway, heading right for her.

"Evie, sweetie." He reached out to pull her into an embrace. "I'm so sorry you've gotten caught in the middle of all this. It was the last thing I wanted."

Evie pulled back, but he wouldn't let go of her hands. She wanted to rip her hands from his grip and slap him, but she realized that such an approach would probably not end well for any of them.

"She doesn't want to talk to you. Not yet."

He shook his head. "Yeah, I got that."

"You should go."

He pulled her hands to his mouth, then sucked one of her knuckles into his mouth, dragging his tongue back and forth across it.

"Are you crazy?" Evie yanked her hands from his and scanned the front of the house. "You think your wife isn't watching from the windows?" She walked to the far side of car, although she wasn't sure whether she was trying to put distance between her and her brother-in-law or her and the house.

He followed her. "I don't care. Besides, if she wants a divorce, then we can be together."

Evie spun around and thrust both hands against his chest. "Jesus! Get over yourself. There is never going to be anything between us. How many times do I have to tell you that?"

She saw the twitch in his jawline and knew she had pushed too far, too fast. She reached down to grasp the car handle, preparing herself to make a mad dash, running him over if need be. Liz was in the house. She would be safe as long as she stayed inside. But Evie was out here, exposed.

"Listen, I think there's something between us."

"There's not!"

He held up a hand to stop her from arguing further.

"I propose we find out for sure, once and for all."

Evie scoffed at him, trying to ignore the visions racing through her head of what he was proposing. None of them were particularly appealing.

"A simple kiss. Just once. If you feel nothing, no sparks, I will walk away forever."

"Not a chance."

"C'mon, Eve. Where's your sense of adventure?"

"Where's your sense of loyalty?"

Her chin jutted out in defiance, and Evie realized too late that it created the opening he'd been waiting for. His lips crushed hers, and he pushed her against the car, holding her in place with his full weight. Her arms were trapped awkwardly between them, giving her no leverage to fight him off, and the door handle dug painfully into her back, disrupting her balance.

She tried to turn her face away from his, but his hand snaked around the back of her neck, holding her head in a vice-like grip.

He was too strong to get away from, so Evie resigned herself to the kiss. He wasn't a bad kisser, but there was definitely no spark. She just needed to endure it for a few more seconds and she would be free of him. She would get away from all of it—her brother-in-law, Liz, Jonathan and his...whatever. She would go somewhere that no one could find her. She would start over, maybe get a teaching certificate and teach art to inner-city kids. A big city would be perfect. She could lose herself in the throng, never to be bothered again.

He wasn't ending the kiss, and Evie's anger was returning. She tried to remain calm, telling herself that he'd have to stop eventually and then she could walk away. When she felt his hand on her thigh, her panic nearly choked her. He had lifted her skirt and was sliding his hand higher. Soon he would discover that she had gone to the dance with the full intention of proving to Jonathan that she was upholding the "commando" agreement. She squirmed against him, but the movement only seemed to embolden him.

Evie realized she had seriously underestimated the situation. She had to act fast to stop him. She stopped fighting and waited for the right moment, trying to ignore how quickly his hand was moving.

She knew the second he realized she wasn't wearing panties and took full advantage of his shock, biting down as hard as she could on his bottom lip. He screamed and jerked back, but she refused to let go until she tasted blood. Finally free, he pulled back from her.

"Jesus, you psychotic bitch!" He wiped at his mouth, then stared at the blood on his hand. "What kind of sick game are you playing?"

Evie barked out a laugh.

He glared at her. "I came out here to fix things and this is what you do?" He spun around, putting several feet between them

Confused about what new game he was trying to play, Evie crossed her arms tightly.

His back was still to her when he spoke again. "You—you I'll talk to, but not your whore of a sister."

Evie's stomach dropped. She turned to see Liz standing on the steps, staring at her with a black expression.

"It was you." Liz's voice was cold, calm—too calm.

Evie forgot how to breathe. She tried to answer, to explain everything, but only squeaks came out. She shook her head, but Liz had already turned her attention to her husband.

"My sister? Really?"

"Liz, honey, she threw herself at me. I fought her off, but I didn't want to tell you. I thought it might hurt you."

Liz sneered in disgust. "Oh, please, Nathan!"

"Nathan?"

Evie turned to see Jonathan walking up the lane, his truck parked at the very end. Her head spun, and she leaned against the car. How much had he seen? But why was he here? Had he brought his girlfriend along? Evie gripped the roof of the car, desperate not to vomit or faint or turn into a puddle of quivering jelly.

"As in Evie's boss Nathan?"

Nathan eyed Jonathan. "Boss. Brother-in-law. What's it to you?"

Jonathan's step faltered. He glanced at Liz. "This piece of work is your husband?"

"Ex-husband."

Jonathan nodded once. "You sure about that?"

"Who is this guy?" Nathan was shouting now, which matched the pounding in Evie's head.

Liz smiled. "Absolutely."

Jonathan slammed a fist into Nathan's gut, and Nathan howled as he fell to the ground. Jonathan didn't give him a chance to recover. He hefted the other man up and half-carried him to his rental car, shoving him into the driver's seat. Nathan started to protest, but Jonathan leaned in and said something that Evie couldn't hear. A moment later, they all watched as Nathan backed down the lane and drove away.

"Nicely done, farm boy," Liz said.

"I don't think he'll be back, but if he is that stupid—"

"Don't worry. I've got the sheriff on speed dial." Liz glanced at Evie. "I'll leave you two alone."

Jonathan tipped an imaginary hat at her, then walked around the back of Evie's car. He didn't come alongside it, though, instead standing by the trunk and staring down the lane, his hands still clenched in fists. "You okay?"

He wouldn't look at her. She wanted to rush to him and explain everything, but her legs were still shaking from everything that had happened. He stood, waiting for her answer, but otherwise cold and distant.

Evie felt heat rising through her body—and not the kind of heat he generally created. He was angry at her? After she'd caught him blowing kisses at that Alex woman? So now he'd caught her in a compromising position with Nathan—a man he knew she was avoiding and clearly had no feelings for—and he was passing judgment on her? It took every ounce of strength not to screech at him.

"Yes, thank you." She was impressed by how calm she sounded.

He waited a second, then nodded almost imperceptibly before walking back to his truck and driving away, never once looking back at her.

Evie watched the lights of the truck disappear into the darkness. Then she finally screeched.

Chapter Fourteen

Jonathan drove home slowly, trying to sort through what he'd just witnessed, but no matter how he approached it, he couldn't ignore the fact that Evie had been kissing another man. It hadn't been a quick kiss either, and they'd been kissing while Liz was inside. He just couldn't wrap his head around all the implications.

When he pulled up next to the house, he saw a light on inside. Susannah's truck was gone. So was Daniel's. He turned off the engine and sat in the truck for a moment, listening for raised voices. The last thing he wanted to do was walk in on a fight between Andrew and Lucas. But no matter how hard he tried to focus, he couldn't hear anything except Evie's calm, confident voice, telling him she was okay.

Jonathan slid out of the truck and dragged himself up the steps to the back door. He turned the handle, cracked the door open, then listened once more for any indication of a fight. Hearing nothing but the crickets in the surrounding fields, he stepped into the house. A pang of concern shot through him. What if the fight was over and the body already buried? He didn't think his brothers would ever intentionally take it that far, but with Andrew's temper and Lucas' questionable mental state, it was very possible Jonathan was about to walk into a bloodbath.

The unnatural silence in the house was getting to Jonathan. It was as if the house was even holding its breath, waiting to learn the ultimate outcome. The floor wasn't squeaking as it normally did; even the constant hum of the refrigerator seemed more muted than usual. Jonathan held his breath and listened once again.

A chair spring squeaked, and Jonathan jerked back, bumping up against the kitchen table.

"In here." Lucas' voice was soft, but carried through to the kitchen as if he were standing next to Jonathan.

The younger Clark brother shuffled toward the living room doorway, peeking inside for any signs of a struggle. He sighed loudly when he saw none. Lucas was sitting in a recliner, reading a newspaper. "Is Andrew around?"

"Sleeping." Lucas didn't bother to look up from the paper.

Jonathan hovered in the doorway. "So, um, did you guys work everything out?"

"Yes."

Jonathan waited. He rubbed at a spot on the doorjamb with his thumb, dragging grease or dirt along his thumb's path. When he pulled his hand back, he saw a black mark covering the length of his upper thumb. He tried to rub it off, but it spread over his skin. He rubbed his hand along his jeans, turning back to Lucas, who was watching him over the top of the newspaper.

Lucas folded the newspaper, dropped it on the coffee table, then sat back in the recliner, watching Jonathan.

Jonathan flashed what he hoped would pass for a smile. "Well, I guess I'd better—"

"Sit."

He dropped to the edge of the couch. "What's up?"

"You tell me."

Jonathan opened his mouth to offer up his usual nonchalant reply, then snapped it shut again. He plucked at a random hair stuck to his jeans. Lucas was talking to him—to everyone—for the first time in almost a decade. So why was he so anxious to get away from him? Now was his chance to ask his brother any of the millions of questions he'd been unable to ask all these years, like what they were going to do about Andrew's shenanigans. And the farm— were they going in the right direction? Dad had always taken care of long-term planning, but now he was gone. How did Lucas deal with missing Mom and Dad? What about being a father—what was that like? And what had he seen in Afghanistan?

He brushed the hair onto the floor and sneaked a glance at his older brother, knowing that any one of those questions could easily send him back to his fortress of silence. So what should he say to him now?

"What's her name?"

Jonathan's head jerked up. "Her name?"

Lucas stared back, waiting.

"Evie—Evelyn." Jonathan shrugged. "She's nobody, though. Not anymore."

Lucas raised his eyebrows in a silent question.

"She, uh, has a complicated history."

Lucas snorted and shook his head.

"I know, I know," Jonathan said, holding up a hand to ward off the expected comments. "Everyone has a history, but hers is particularly complicated."

Lucas continued to watch Jonathan, waiting for him to offer up more information. Jonathan squirmed under his brother's gaze, wondering how much of Evie's story he should share. As upset as he was about what he witnessed earlier that night, he didn't want to create problems for her by sharing his intimate knowledge of her life with outsiders. Then again, Lucas was not the kind to spread rumors. Even now that he was talking again, he barely said more than a handful of words. Jonathan couldn't envision him suddenly gushing forth with details about a family he'd never met. That just wasn't who Lucas was.

Jonathan took a deep breath. "She told me that her boss had a thing for her. And he did seem to be pretty persistent after she quit." He remembered their kiss at the Porterhouse and smiled. Then a vision of her kissing Nathan popped into his mind and his smile soured. "Turns out her boss was actually her brother-in-law, who I discovered her kissing tonight when I went over to explain that Alex was Daniel's girlfriend, not mine."

Lucas furrowed his brow in confusion.

"Yeah, it's all so complicated, I don't know exactly what's going on." Jonathan rubbed his temple. "Look, I met this girl—Evie—at Porters' pond. And she's...she's incredible. I mean, she's fearless. And intense. And spontaneous. She's an amazing artist, and she has no clue how utterly beautiful she is, which just makes her even more gorgeous, you know? And I just want to be around her all the time. I'm not talking only about the sex here—although, yeah...whoa. But just being around her, I don't know how to explain it."

"But?"

Jonathan threw his hands in the air and stood up. He paced the length of the sofa several times, then plopped back down. "But, I don't know. She saw me and Alex Porter teasing each other—and we were just doing it to mess with Daniel—but Evie might have thought it was something more. I dunno. Honestly, I don't know what she thinks because when I went over to talk to her, she was kissing Nathan, her boss slash brother-in-law. I mean, jeez, I thought we had a messed up family, ya know?"

Lucas leaned back and frowned in disapproval.

"Oh, man, I didn't mean it like that, Lucas."

Lucas drummed his fingers on the armrest.

"They were kissing. He pulled back, and he was angry. Then he was talking to Evie's sister, calling Evie a whore—which makes no sense. Believe me, she's no whore. There were plenty of times when we could have—" He snapped his mouth shut, hoping that the heat in his face wasn't visible.

A half-smile flittered across Lucas' face. "Then?"

"Then I punched him."

Lucas scowled, but Jonathan shrugged.

"He deserved it, trust me. And then I put him in his car and he left."

"And Evie?"

Jonathan shrugged.

Lucas eyed Jonathan for a moment. "So you're saying that this Nathan guy left, but Evie didn't. She stayed?"

"Yep."

Lucas picked up the newspaper again. "You're a fool."

"Gee, thanks for the support."

"You kicked the guy to the curb and she didn't complain. Think about it."

Twenty minutes later, Jonathan was pounding on Evie's door. "It's me, Evie. Open up. I want to talk."

Liz pulled the door open, shaking her head. "She's gone for good, as usual." Liz opened the screen door and motioned him inside, but Jonathan remained on the porch.

"What do you mean? Where is she?"

"She packed a bag and left not five minutes after you did. This is what Evie does, runs away."

"Where to?"

Liz shrugged. "She'll eventually let me know where's she's at, what new town she's found."

Jonathan felt like he'd been sucker-punched. He stumbled down the steps and back to his truck, surprised that his feet could obey the jumbled commands in his brain. *She's gone? Just like that? What about her house? Her things?* A coldness crept into his chest when he remembered how easily she'd quit her job in Denver—she'd been there how many years?—and decided to stay in Bender after a five-minute meeting with him. If it had been that easy to leave her life in Denver, how much easier would it be to leave Bender, where she had no real friends, no job? Hell, she'd only been in town for a few weeks, a month or so at most. He reached out to lean against his truck. Would he ever see her again?

"Do you love her?"

He glanced back at Liz. "I don't see how that matters—"

"I'm not asking if you want to marry her or spend your life with her, just do you love her?"

He closed his eyes, willing himself to deny it. "Yes."

"Good."

When he opened his eyes, Liz was closing the door. "So where can I find her?"

Liz paused, then smiled. "Wherever she wants to be found."

Chapter Fifteen

Evie looked through the small office's tinted window. The bank officer was so low on the totem pole that his office looked out onto the parking lot. Still, Evie didn't mind. Anything was better than watching the man wrinkle his forehead and sigh at the computer.

She could smell the tar from the newly paved parking lot, and it was already starting to give her a headache. She couldn't imagine how much worse it would be by the afternoon. Even in November, the Arizona sun was intense. She thought spending the winter in a sunny locale would be just the boost she needed to pull herself out of her funk, but the bank's Christmas decorations looked sorely out of place when it was seventy-five degrees out and the chance of snow was non-existent. Granted, she still had more than a month before her favorite holiday, but she wasn't sure she could endure day after day of knowing that she wouldn't see any of the white stuff this year. It would be her first Christmas without snow. The thought sent her even deeper into her gloom, and she turned away from the window.

The bank officer sighed again, a little too dramatically in Evie's opinion, and she realized that he'd been putting on a show—that he knew he wouldn't be able to help her before she even sat down. She'd wasted a plunging neckline on this man. He clearly didn't see it that way, as he glanced up, pausing a few seconds on her bosom while he licked his lips before finally meeting her eyes.

"I'm real sorry, Miss Jacobs. I just don't see how I can help. Your bank in Nebraska refuses to let the transfer go through."

Evie flashed him a tight smile. "Jacobson."

"Huh?"

"It's Jacobson, not Jacobs."

He traced his index finger across the computer screen. "Oh right, right. I see here. Jacobson." He nodded at her.

Evie stood. "Well, at least you confirmed my last name is correct."

She knew the sarcasm was lost on him as he was staring at her cleavage again. She planted her hands on his desk and leaned over until she was practically falling out of her shirt. The bank officer was smacking his lips, making crude slurping sounds. His eyes never left her chest.

"I'd really, really like to thank you for your help." Evie made her voice soft, breathless, sultry. She ran a finger along the top of her blouse, pulling it down just enough to show off the lace of her bra. "Would that be okay?"

The bank officer glanced at the office door, then back at her chest. He was almost hyperventilating with excitement. He pushed back from his desk, but Evie held up a hand.

"No, you stay right there." She stood upright and took slow backward steps toward the door. "I want you fully ready for me. Can you do that?"

His head bobbed up and down in response.

"You sure?" She was halfway to the office door but was still using her soft, sultry voice. "Can you show me—that you're ready for me?" When he faltered, looking back to the door, Evie was ready. "Don't worry. I won't let anyone else see. Just me." She unbuttoned her blouse, revealing the skimpiest lace bra she owned. "Aren't you gonna join me?"

His attention was immediately back on her, and she looked at his bulging crotch while slowly dragging her tongue across her upper lip. He took the hint and fumbled with his trousers until the bulge surged just above his shorts.

It was Evie's turn to smack her lips as she reached back toward the door. "I'm gonna need a minute to catch up with you. You don't want to hurt me, do you?"

He shook his head, but she caught the gleam in his eye suggesting that he wanted to do just that.

"Okay, then, big boy. Tell you what. You close your eyes and count to ten—and no peeking!"

The door was almost closed now, and he was becoming more emboldened, pulling himself further from his pants to show just how excited he was. Evie nodded in appreciation.

"That's right, you're gonna give it all to me—after you count to ten. And if you don't peek, I will let you do whatever you want to me. Agreed?"

He was shaking with excitement, and she worried he would lose control before he got to ten. He closed his eyes and counted. "One...two..."

Evie slipped through the door, careful not to let it close, and moved down the hallway while buttoning her blouse. She found a male bank employee filling out forms at a large desk.

"Excuse me." Evie waited for him to look up from his forms. "I don't mean to be a bother to anyone, but I was just speaking to..." She motioned to the closed door.

"Mr. Schneider?"

"Yes, that's him." Evie flashed a smile of thanks. "Anyway, he's doing the most peculiar thing now, just randomly counting. Maybe you should check on him?"

To his credit, the man kept the reassuring smile firmly in place as he stepped past Evie to open the door. Evie raced out of the bank. The shouting started before Evie hit the front doors, and by the time she was on the sidewalk, she was laughing so hard she had to pause to try and catch her breath.

She spun around to face the bank. "Serves you right, you pervert!"

Several passersby slowed to stare, and Evie bowed deeply.

Her spirits remained high until she got to her car on the far side of the customer parking lot. When she looked in the rearview mirror to back out of the parking space, she thought she saw a familiar truck driving by. She twisted in the seat, her heart thumping in her chest.

It wasn't him.

The Arizona plates on the truck should have been a dead giveaway, but Evie still held her breath until she saw an old man get out, his long white hair pulled back into a ponytail that hung halfway down his back.

"Definitely not him."

She threw the car in reverse and backed out, then pulled out into westbound traffic.

"Sixty-seven days and you still think you see him everywhere. Better get over him, Ms. Evelyn Jacobson, or people might think you've gone off the deep end."

She glanced at her reflection in the rearview mirror and snorted. "As if you haven't already."

Her apartment was actually a duplex, where she lived in the western half of a single-story house. The other tenant was a sophomore at the University of Arizona who apparently had directionally challenged friends because they continued to park in her driveway. Today was no exception. She swore under her breath. The street was a no-parking zone, and she'd already gotten a ticket for parking there while she waited for her neighbor's friend to move his car. She couldn't afford another one, especially as she was down to her last bit of cash. She decided that two could play this game and pulled into her neighbor's empty lane.

"Really, frat boy? Park in my driveway when yours is wide open?" She got out of her car and walked across the front yard, her heels sinking in the sand while she mumbled about the country's failing educational system. Once inside, she dropped her purse on the kitchen table and kicked off her shoes. She was changing into a pair of jeans and an old t-shirt when she heard frat boy's little sports car pull up outside. She hurried to the living room, about to run outside to move her car for him, then stopped. She'd make him come to her, just like he'd always done. She grabbed a soda from the fridge to celebrate the ingenuity of her plan.

When the knock sounded on her door, she smiled. "Just a minute!" She finished the rest of her soda, then walked to the door.

"Guess what I got?"

Evie felt like she'd been punched in the gut. She stumbled backwards, her head swimming as she realized—too late—that she hadn't closed the door.

Nathan followed her inside, closing the door behind him before rushing to her side. "Evie, you okay? You look like you just saw a ghost!"

"What—what are you doing here?" She pushed away from him and moved to stand in front of the sink, where she could lean against the counter until her knees stopped shaking.

"I came to show you the good news." He held up a packet of paper. "We're all good, baby."

"Look, I don't know what you're—"

"The divorce." He handed the papers to her. "I mean, it's not final yet, but at least it's a start."

Evie tried to focus on the papers in her hands, but her brain was screaming at her to get out of the apartment, get away from Nathan. *How did he find me, anyway?*

Nathan stepped up behind her, sliding his hands around her waist and resting his chin on her shoulder. "Now it can be just you and me."

Jesus, he was delusional. If anyone's gone off the deep end, it's him—way, way off.

She needed to put some distance between them, give herself a chance to get away. She'd go next door to frat boy. Surely he could take Nathan. She tried to pull away from him, but his embrace tightened. "Nathan."

"Hmm?"

"You know I can't deal with people reading over my shoulder."

"Oh, right." He pulled his face back and buried it in her hair. "Better?"

"Not really, no."

He sighed dramatically, then stepped back from her. "Fine, fine. Got anything to drink?"

She motioned to the fridge while pretending to be engrossed in the papers. She moved closer to the table and further from Nathan. The papers were, in fact, divorce papers, but she noted that Liz was suing Nathan for divorce. "Good for you," she mumbled.

"What's that?"

Evie shook her head. "Nothing. Oh, but hey, how did you find me, anyway?"

Nathan beamed with pride. "You still have a company cell phone."

She barely stopped the groan from escaping her lips. "So why now, after all this time?"

He poured a soda into a glass and took a long swig. "I told you. I wanted to share the good news."

She knew he was lying, which made her even more nervous. "These papers are dated two months ago."

He finished the rest of the soda, watching her over the rim of the glass. It took all her determination not to squirm and look away.

"Fine, fine. I wasn't going to tell you this." He set the empty glass in the sink and moved to stand next to her. "I was afraid it made me look weak."

"You? Never." Evie forced a smile, realizing she had maneuvered herself so that Nathan was now standing between her and her purse. *Well, that was brilliant.*

He took off his jacket and hung it over the back of the chair, then sat down. "And that's how I know you love me, Evie."

Bile rose in her throat, but she kept her smile in place.

"Actually, it was that local kid—what was his name?"

Evie's chest tightened as he reached back into his jacket pocket, then dumped the contents on the table in front of them. He brushed aside several crumpled pieces of paper before plucking one out of the pile and smoothing it out on the table. "Jonathan Clark."

A chill ran down her spine. "Jonathan?" Her voice cracked, and she cleared her throat. "What about him?"

"He's the one who told me to come find you. Said he made a terrible mistake, misinterpreted everything that night—you know, you really gave a good show. My lip—"

"He said what?" Her calm voice belied the turmoil raging inside her. Jonathan sent Nathan to find her? *Nathan?!*

"Don't worry, Evie." He grasped her hands in his. "It's all good now."

"Get your hands off me."

Nathan frowned. "What's your problem? After all I did to find you—"

"All you did? All you did!" She was shrieking, unable to control her emotions. "You sick, pathetic bastard. There was never anything between us. There never will be. All you did was stalk me and harass me and then assault me!" She jumped up from the table and threw open the door. "Get out!"

"No." He folded his arms over his chest. "I'm not going anywhere until we work this out."

She grabbed her purse off the counter. "Fine, I'll leave." She slammed the door behind her, ignoring the fact that she was still barefoot. When she rounded the corner to cross the front yard to her car, he heart sank. It wasn't frat boy's car parked behind hers in the driveway. It was Nathan's sedan.

She spun around to find Nathan, his head cocked to the side and a smirk on his lips. "Move your car."

He grabbed her arm and hissed, "I told you. I'm not going anywhere until we work this out."

His grip tightened until Evie thought he might snap her bone. She sneered at him. "Oh, we'll work it out all right." She jerked her free hand upward, connecting the base of her palm with his chin and snapping his head back. His grip on her arm loosened, and she grabbed his shoulders and pulled down as she lifted her knee, connecting squarely with his groin.

He howled in pain and fell into the sandy yard. Evie bent over him, digging through his pockets until she found his keys. "I'm going to borrow your car for a bit. I'll have someone return it." She stood and kicked sand in face. She wanted to do more to hurt him, but that would have to suffice. "If I ever see you again, I will kill you."

She didn't know where she planned on going once she got in Nathan's car. She just drove, letting the anger wash over her. She gripped the steering wheel so tightly her fingernails left scars in the soft plastic covering. When she finally calmed down enough to note where she was, she realized she was on the interstate headed east and was halfway to New Mexico already. She smiled.

"So, Mr. Clark, you want to send Nathan after me? Let me tell you what I think about that." She'd spend the next twenty hours fine-tuning just what she would say to Jonathan Clark. She was certainly going to give him a piece of her mind. Maybe even several pieces.

Chapter Sixteen

When Jonathan got the call from Liz, he was only an hour from the Andersen County Courthouse, which was located near the border with Colorado. He'd spent the last few weeks haunting Denver, trying to find some hint of Evie, but she clearly didn't want to be found, so he gave up and was heading back home when he got the call. When Liz explained that Evie was back in Nebraska, he thought he'd finally caught a break and had agreed to go rescue her.

He'd regretted agreeing before he got the full story. Evie had been picked up for speeding. In Nathan's car, which he had called in as stolen. After getting that little tidbit of information, Jonathan had stopped at a greasy spoon near the interstate and ordered a cup of coffee while he tried to figure out if he'd been played for a fool all along. If she'd been driving Nathan's car, clearly they were together somewhere, wherever that might be. But that didn't fit with the way Evie had spoken about her boss, the way that she'd ignored his calls, or Nathan calling in his car as stolen. Had she just been using Jonathan to make Nathan jealous?

He'd spent the night at a nearby hotel, getting no sleep as he reexamined everything he knew about Evie, which admittedly wasn't much. But he couldn't shake the feeling that he knew her, the real her—the Evie who loved spontaneity and hated commitment. From what he'd learned about Nathan while in Denver, the two of them would mix as well as oil and water. He'd checked out of the hotel, realizing that he had to get answers, and the only way to do that was to confront Evie.

Now, as Jonathan pulled into the county seat—a town of fewer than four hundred people—he slowed his truck to a crawl, wondering if he was about to walk into the middle of a lover's spat. He parked in front of a small single-story building with the word "courthouse" painted in black on the window. He was sliding out of the truck when the courthouse door opened and a large pot-bellied man emerged.

The man was wearing blue-black jeans and a dark brown sheriff's shirt, its sleeves rolled up to his elbows. "You from Sweeney and Appleton?"

Jonathan nodded, and the sheriff smiled in relief, sticking a giant hand out to shake Jonathan's.

"Thank the lord almighty. I'm not sure I can take another minute with her." The sheriff didn't seem too eager to return indoors, despite the bracing chill in the air that made Jonathan thankful he was wearing his coat.

"Mr. Sweeney was supposed to wire the bail money to the bank."

The sheriff was already shaking his head. "Ain't no bail. Got a hold of the car's owner and convinced him to drop the theft charges."

Jonathan frowned. So it was a lover's spat, and soon she would be reunited with Nathan. "You release her?"

"Not yet. Been waiting for you."

"Me?"

"Car's impounded until Mr. Miller can get here, which might not be for a few days. She's got no transportation and, quite frankly, I want her out of my town." He smiled, showing a row of tobacco-stained teeth. "Thought about taking her to the county line myself, but I'm not convinced she's got it all going on upstairs, if you know what I mean."

The sheriff closed his eyes and took a deep breath, as if trying to steel himself. Jonathan glanced back at his truck, wondering if he should get back in and head home now, while he still had the chance. Somehow he didn't think the sheriff would let him get away, even if it meant chasing him halfway across the state to drag him back. He shoved his hands in his coat pockets. Better to get it over with now and be done with it. Surely he could survive a few hours in the truck with her.

The sheriff clapped Jonathan on the back. "You ready, Mr. Sweeney? Or is it Mr. Appleton?"

"Actually, it's Clark—Jonathan Clark." He saw the hesitation in the sheriff's eyes. "Is that going to be a problem?"

"Son, I don't care if you claim to be Abraham Lincoln and wear a pink polka-dotted tutu. She's leaving with you."

"She might argue that point."

The sheriff nodded. "I figured. I can take care of that. Sweeney and Appleton must be paying you a small fortune to take care of this little filly."

Jonathan started to correct him, then pulled his coat tighter about him and looked down as he shuffled his feet.

The sheriff erupted into a throaty laugh that ended in a coughing fit. When he could finally speak again, he was wiping tears from his eyes. "Son, I had the same problem when I met Mrs. Jackson. She had me tripping over my own two feet for years before I learned how to manage her." He broke out laughing again. "Oh, who am I kidding? Never did learn how to manage her, but I've had a hell of a ride while trying. Best thirty-six years of my life." He winked. "Worst thirty-six as well."

He pulled open the door, and they heard a loud, off-key voice singing "Nobody Knows the Trouble I've Seen." The sheriff chuckled. "Oh, I don't envy you with this one. Not one bit."

He pointed to a chair and nodded at Jonathan to sit before walking through a doorway behind the desk. Jonathan considered sitting for all of about three seconds. Being on his feet would give him more options if Evie did something rash, and with Evie, everything she did was rash. He assumed that sitting in the county jail for almost a full day would make her even harder to deal with, and based on what he overheard from the back room, his assumption was well founded.

"Your ride's here, missy."

"Oh, so you finally got the ransom you demanded? What idiot did you find to escort me from this hell hole?"

Jonathan cringed. He was tempted to leave now that the sheriff was distracted. What was the worst that could happen?

When Evie stepped through the doorway, all thoughts of leaving evaporated. The minute she saw

Jonathan, she stopped. The sheriff, walking behind her, had to pull up abruptly to keep from running into her.

Jonathan told himself to look away, but no matter how loud the voice in his head screamed, he couldn't stop staring. Spending a night in jail made most people look the worse for wear, but Evie's unbrushed hair, slightly puffy eyes, and wrinkled t-shirt reminded him too much of what she looked like the morning after a night of lovemaking. Visions of their night together flooded his mind, and he noticed a slight flush in Evie's cheeks, as if she were reliving the same memories. That thought nearly brought Jonathan to his knees, and he absently wondered how much the sheriff would charge them to use his cell for a few hours of alone time.

Jonathan grimaced, forcing himself to look away. How in the hell would he survive five minutes alone with her in his truck? A flash of color caught his attention and he glanced at Evie's feet, which were covered in bright pink bunny slippers. He looked from the smiling bunny face and floppy ears to Evie's scowl and burst out in a rumbling laughter that echoed off the walls.

It was the wrong thing to do.

Chapter Seventeen

Evie stared slack-jawed at Jonathan. His grimace had been bad enough, telling her exactly what he thought of her. His laughter was just downright rude. What was it about her predicament that he found so funny?

When he didn't stop laughing, she crossed her arms tightly, barely controlling her anger. The sheriff pulled at her elbow, trying to move her from the doorway, but she spun around to walk back to the cell.

The sheriff's grip on her elbow tightened. "Not a chance in hell, missy." He pulled her around and dragged her closer to Jonathan. "Son, you're not earning any brownie points here, and if Mrs. Jackson found out you were laughing at her slippers, she'd have your hide."

Jonathan instantly sobered. "Where are her shoes?"

The sheriff shrugged. "That is a discussion for the road." He ushered them toward the front door.

"Wait, you can't make me go with him." Evie fought a rising panic at the thought of being alone with Jonathan.

"Actually, I can, missy. One of the conditions of your release is that you answer to Mr. Clark."

She cast a sidelong glance at Jonathan. "Answer to him?"

"Yep." The sheriff handed her things to Jonathan. "He's responsible for you, so I expect you to do what he says."

She heard Jonathan stifle a groan and realized that he was just as unhappy with this arrangement as she was. Part of her was relieved. If he didn't want to be responsible for her, they could part ways fairly quickly. Another part of her was hurt by his reaction. She stuffed that part deep down inside her. She didn't want to hear from it.

Evie nodded at the sheriff. "For how long?

The sheriff rubbed a hand across his face, but Evie saw the smile he was trying to hide. What was he up to?

"Well, missy, grand theft is a serious charge. Until we get it all worked out, you are technically still a prisoner of the state of Nebraska."

She held up her hands in mock surrender. "Fine, fine. Whatever. This will all get resolved as soon as you talk to Nathan, and then I am going to put this whole state behind me. Forever." She looked at Jonathan, a sour expression on her face. "Shall we?"

She walked out of the courthouse ahead of him, trying to ignore the cold look in his eyes.

Evie sat in the truck, her arms crossed tightly and her hands tucked under her arms. She was freezing, but she refused to admit it. Not to Jonathan, at least. She had driven across several states to lash out at him about Nathan, but somewhere along the way her brain had finally gotten through to her heart. She knew that Nathan was delusional. He spoke in half-truths at best. But she hadn't wanted to go back to Arizona until she was sure Nathan was gone, so she'd kept driving.

She was sitting close enough to Jonathan that she could smell the hints of earthy pastureland on his boots and the crisp detergent used on his jeans. It would be so easy to reach out and run her fingers through his hair and taste the savory heat of his kisses. She felt more miserable now than ever before.

She could tell he didn't want to be around her, much less be responsible for her. His grimaces and groans when the sheriff was explaining the condition of her release made everything all too clear. He was so disgusted by having to come get her that he hadn't looked at her once since they got in the truck, and he hadn't said a single word.

But why had he come?

She stared at the two-lane highway extending for miles before them. Bender was still several hours away. She wasn't sure she could endure the silence without knowing the truth. "I figured the sheriff would just let me go after Mr. Sweeney paid the bail."

She waited for a response, but none came. She tried again.

"So why didn't Mr. Sweeney come get me himself?"

"Mr. Sweeney's a ninety-year-old contract lawyer who can barely get to his office every day, much less drive across the state."

His clipped words should have warned her to drop her attempts at conversation, but talking made her forget how cold she was.

"And Mr. Appleton?"

"Died more than fifteen years ago."

"Oh." She tried to think of a way to continue the conversation, but his body language was screaming at her to leave him alone. He stared at the road, his right arm propped on the steering wheel. She could see the muscles in his jaw straining in their tightness. It was going to be a very long drive back to Bender. "Well, I'll make sure he pays you well for the inconvenience."

He glanced at her now. Had she not been watching him so closely she would have missed it—the look of pure hatred in his eyes.

Chapter Eighteen

Jonathan was gripping the steering wheel so hard his knuckles were white and he was losing feeling in the tips of his fingers. Coming to clean up her mess was truly an inconvenience, especially when all she'd wanted to do was contact Nathan and clear everything up. Well, he'd wanted answers. Now he had them. She didn't care about him, didn't even try to talk to him except to ask about payment for services rendered. She didn't even bother to ask where he was taking her.

Where was he taking her? When he agreed to help out, he'd been so focused on the idea of knowing, once and for all, how she felt that he hadn't even considered what he was supposed to do with her. He'd just assumed she'd go back to Bender, where

Liz was. But what if she wanted to go to Denver and be with Nathan?

Jonathan couldn't bring himself to ask. She was clearly with Nathan. He didn't need her to actually say the words. He didn't think he'd be able to if she did. He certainly wasn't going to take her to Denver and drop her off with her lover. So that left spending five hours in his truck with her, listening to her silence while trying to get the pictures of their night together out of his head.

Dammit, what was wrong with him? She was with Nathan. She'd made her choice. So why was he tormenting himself thinking about exploring her body with his kisses, remembering the subtle saltiness of her skin mingled with the smell of vanilla—a smell he still hadn't discovered the source of—and picturing her in that moment when she experienced the ultimate release?

He couldn't do it. He couldn't survive several hours without touching her. He could barely endure several minutes.

He followed the signs for Ogallala, pulling into the first gas station. When he got out of the truck, he was grateful that Evie made no move to join him. It was his first bit of good luck since she left Bender. His luck continued when he spoke to the clerk inside, who was all too happy to share information with him while batting her heavily lined eyes.

When he returned to his truck, he opened the passenger door and hauled Evie out.

"What the—"

"Here." He held out several slips of paper. "I promised to make sure you got to where you needed to go, and I'm doing that. There's two tickets there, one to Omaha and one—well, the other one heads west." He couldn't look at her so he stared at her bunny slippers instead. "Pick one. But let your sister know when you arrive."

When she didn't take the tickets, he grabbed her hand and slapped the tickets into it. He then slammed the passenger door closed. Finally, he looked at her. Her face was drained of color, and she stared at him.

"Good-bye, Evie."

He hurried to get in the truck before he changed his mind. When he accelerated on the ramp to the interstate, he finally allowed himself to breathe again.

Chapter Nineteen

Evie pulled the blanket back over her head. She was moping, and she knew it. She knew it wasn't healthy, but she didn't care. When she'd escaped from Nathan, her first thought had been to get to Jonathan and give him a piece of her mind. Driving across the eastern plains of Colorado had given her plenty of time to think. Nathan had undoubtedly lied to her, but she continued driving because she realized that he gave her the excuse she needed to head back to Nebraska. And Jonathan.

She'd been so focused on forgetting about Jonathan that she hadn't once stopped to wonder why she should. Why hadn't she tried to find him that night and explain everything to him? He'd obviously left the dance to come to find her, suggesting that maybe she'd overreacted when she saw him with Alex. But she hadn't gone to find Jonathan when she had been caught in a compromising position.

Because running away was her go-to response. It had served her well in the past. It was quick, clean, painless. Usually.

This time, running away had not solved anything. In fact, it had created so many new problems— problems she would never be able to fix. Staying in bed another day would not change anything either.

She dragged herself out from under the blanket and glanced in the large mirror above her dresser. She barely recognized herself. If she was going to force herself to stop moping about Jonathan, the first thing she would have to do is take a shower. She stretched her arms back, then grimaced at her own smell.

"A very long, hot, disinfecting shower."

When she finally made it downstairs, she was wearing clean clothes for the first time in a week and her hair was no longer hanging in stringy clumps around her face. She almost felt human.

Almost.

She walked into the kitchen and stopped when she saw Liz sitting at the table. Evie had been so focused on forgetting Jonathan when she left for Arizona that she'd completely forgotten about how the scene with Nathan might have affected Liz. Luckily, Liz seemed to know all too well that Nathan had fabricated his entire relationship with Evie—at least that was what she implied when she picked Evie up at the bus station in Omaha.

Before she'd even said hello, Liz had looked Evie up and down, then said, "You didn't sleep with him."

It wasn't a question, but Evie had felt the need to convince her sister that she'd had absolutely no interested in Nathan. She'd launched into a long litany of his faults.

Liz had eventually held up a hand to stop her. "I was married to him, you know."

The sisters hadn't spoken the entire ride home or in the week since Evie returned.

Evie cleared her throat. "Um, we okay?"

Liz stood and grabbed a coffee mug from the cupboard. "Now that you've showered? Yeah, we're good."

Evie shifted uncomfortably. "You want to talk about...you know?"

Liz eyed her as she filled the mug with coffee. "You want to talk about your own 'you know'?"

Evie shook her head.

"Good. Then drink your coffee. We've got errands to run today."

The errands turned out to be visiting several antique stores. In the past several months, Liz had developed relationships with most of the store owners, and when the sisters arrived at each store, the owners would pull out the pieces that they'd held back just for Liz. Evie pretended to be interested in the stories the owners shared about pieces of jewelry and serving plates and even a perfectly preserved wedding dress, but her mind continued to wander back to thoughts of Jonathan and how she'd messed everything up so badly.

It was dark by the time they finally started heading home, and Liz pulled in to the Porterhouse Bar, explaining that she didn't feel like cooking tonight. Evie didn't feel much like eating, especially here, but she knew that trying to explain that to Liz would just bring back more memories best left forgotten. This was as good a place as any to start forgetting Jonathan. Time to remove the bandage and check the wound.

It was more like ripping off the bandage and screaming in pain. Alex Porter greeted them at the door. Evie managed not to burst into tears, but only just barely—especially when it turned out that Alex was not only the hostess but also the waitress. And a very chatty one at that.

"I'm so happy you're back." She hugged Evie, then showed them to a booth along the wall. "Johnny's just been a mess since you left. Never seen him like this. It's so not like him."

When she handed them their menus, Liz nodded at the large diamond on Alex's finger. "Holy cow. Looks like you found a keeper."

Alex squealed and held out her hand proudly for both sisters to see. "Can you believe it? He even did it all proper-like and asked my dad for permission."

Evie tried to swallow but her mouth was too dry. Obviously what she'd seen at the dance had been exactly what she thought it was. She finally squeaked out a "congratulations."

Alex sat in the booth next to Evie. "Now, I know we barely know each other, but you're kinda responsible for us getting together, so you absolutely must be in the wedding. I won't take no for an answer."

"I'm—I'm flattered." Evie looked from Alex to Liz and back to Alex. "But I don't think that would be appropriate." Watch the man she loved walk down the aisle with another woman? She'd rather go back to jail. "I'm sure you and Jonathan will have a wonderful wedding, but—"

Alex laughed so loudly that several patrons turned to see the cause of the commotion. Evie shrank back against the booth.

"Sweetie, what on earth makes you think I could ever turn Jonathan's head, especially when he is so totally in love with you?"

Liz leaned over the table. "We saw you at the street dance. We heard him declaring his love for you."

"Oh my goodness!" Alex grabbed Evie's hands. "Did you leave because of me? Because of what you saw? Oh, sweetie. No, no, no. My heart belongs to another Clark brother. Danny's the only man for me. That night at the street dance, Johnny was just teasing Danny."

Evie tried to speak, but nothing happened.

Liz had no such problem. "So you're not marrying Jonathan Clark."

"Goodness, no. Johnny? He's head over heels with Evie. Isn't that why he was in Denver so long?"

Liz frowned. "Denver?"

"Yeah, he was gone for nearly a month. I barely got to see Danny that entire time, he was so busy covering for Johnny." She squeezed Evie's hands. "He went out there for you, right?"

Evie shook her head.

Alex frowned, looking between the two sisters.

Evie cleared her throat. "I don't know why he went to Denver, but it certainly wasn't for me. He— he hates me." Her voice cracked and she bit her lip to keep from crying.

"No, ma'am, he certainly does not." Alex leaned closer, as if sharing a secret. "I've never seen that boy so messed up as when you left, and I've known him my entire life."

Evie shrugged. "Something changed, then."

"Why would you say that?"

This time she couldn't stop the tears from welling up in her eyes. She grabbed a napkin and dabbed at them before continuing. "Because he abandoned me at a gas station, with no shoes, no coat, and no money, just two bus tickets."

Liz and Alex glanced at each other, then looked at Evie and shouted in unison, "He did what?!"

Evie explained how she'd left Arizona in such a hurry, without shoes or even a jacket, and with less than a hundred dollars in her bank account. When she'd been stopped for speeding and they ran the tags, she'd been taken to the city jail until they could sort through the car's ownership. "They even gave me a pair of these stupid bunny slippers to wear around the cell. So can you imagine when I saw Jonathan—someone I was not expecting at all—and I am standing there, not having showered in days and wearing pink bunny slippers... Well, he made it perfectly clear that coming to help me was a huge inconvenience, that he didn't want to be there and didn't want to be around me. So when the sheriff let me go, Jonathan took me to the nearest town, handed me two tickets, and left."

Alex was scowling. "Jonathan Clark left you in a strange town, with no coat, no money, and wearing bunny slippers?"

Evie nodded.

"That son of a bitch." Alex glanced up when the door to the bar opened and several new people walked in. "Honey, you sit tight. Lemme seat these people, then we're gonna figure out just what to do with Mr. Clark."

After Alex headed for the door, Liz reached across the table to pat Evie's hands.

"Evie, sweetie, something doesn't feel right."

"What do you mean?" Evie sniffled, grabbing a napkin to wipe at her nose.

"It's just, when I called him, he seemed more than happy to go get you." Liz frowned. "Until I told him about Nathan's car."

"I swear, I did not tell Nathan where I was."

Liz waved her protests away. "I've had plenty of time for my own reflections, and I know Nathan has more than a few screws loose, especially when it comes to you. I just wish you had told me he was harassing you."

Evie hunched over the table. "I wanted you to be happy."

A commotion erupted by the front door, and both sisters turned to see Alex facing off against a group of men, both hands planted firmly on her hips.

"You don't believe me? She's right there." Alex pointed toward Evie. "Just go ask her."

Several people turned toward Evie and Liz, but Evie fixated on only one of them: Jonathan Clark. He scowled at her, then stormed across the bar. Evie scrambled out of the booth. If she was going to face off against him here, in public, she didn't want to feel cornered in a booth.

"Just what the hell do you think you're doing spreading lies about me?"

His snarl made her flinch, but she refused to look away.

"I told Alex exactly how you left me."

"I left you with two bus tickets. Your choice. You could go anywhere you wanted and live your life." He threw his hands in the air. "Options! I gave you options, but you're telling people I stranded you?"

Evie's own anger flared, and she took a step toward him. "You left me in a strange town in the middle of November with no money, no coat, and I was wearing bunny slippers!" She was screaming by the time she finished.

"How the hell was I supposed to know you didn't have any money?"

"Oh, I don't know. Maybe if you had talked to me or even looked at me, you would have figured it out. But you didn't ask. No, you just groaned about having to come get me—which I didn't ask you to do, by the way."

"Someone had to get you, and your precious Nathan was nowhere to be found, was he?"

Liz moved to stand next to Evie. "I feel like I should interject here—"

Without taking their eyes off one another, Evie and Jonathan both said, "Sit down!"

Liz held up her hands and moved to stand next to Alex and Daniel.

Evie took a breath to calm herself, then spoke in a quiet voice. "You know there was never anything between me and Nathan."

"Really?" Jonathan leaned forward until he was just inches from Evie. "That's not what it looked like to me."

"And just what did it look like? To your trained eye."

He returned her sarcasm with a contemptuous smile of his own. "I saw you kissing him, all cozy and pressed up against your car."

"Pressed up, huh? Try pinned. Yeah, that's right, pinned." Evie crossed her arms and jutted her chin out in defiance. When he didn't respond, she continued. "And then I bit his lip—so hard I got blood stains on my dress."

"I can vouch for that one," Liz called out over Jonathan's shoulder. "Asshole sent me the ER bill."

Jonathan stared at Evie, but she could see that the anger was gone from his eyes. His face was still guarded, though. He didn't trust her.

Evie dropped her chin to her chest and heaved a sigh. She was suddenly more exhausted than she'd ever been, and she didn't want to fight anymore. When she looked back up at him, she saw his mouth twitch in a half-smile before he could hide it.

She paused a moment before speaking, trying to collect her thoughts. When she spoke again, it was only for him to hear. "Look, I don't want to fight. We had some fun, now we've moved on. Let's just call it friends and be done."

"There you go again, running away."

Evie scowled at him. She was trying to end this gracefully, but he wasn't taking the hint. "Yeah, so I run away. Just like before. I ran away from you, Jonathan Clark. And then I came back." She poked him in the chest to punctuate her last words.

"That's right. You came back!"

"That's what I said. I came back. For you."

"For me? In a stolen car—with no money, no clothes, no shoes, no nothing. But you expect me to believe you came back for me and that you weren't just running away from some other new mess you'd gotten yourself into."

Evie screamed, "Yes!"

"And why should I believe you?"

"Because I love you!"

"Well, good! Because I love you too!"

They stared at each other in silence, both breathing heavily from the shouting. The patrons in the bar around them were all silent, watching the drama unfold.

Daniel cleared his throat. "Jesus, man, kiss her already."

In an instant, Evie's heavy breathing shifted from exertion to excitement as she realized what Jonathan had just said. *He loves me!* Could they move past their history and build something real? She was willing to try. In fact, she was willing to bet her entire life on being with Jonathan. But she needed a sign from him—something, anything to let her know that he was interested in trying as well.

And then Jonathan spun around and stormed out the front door.

Evie stared after him, feeling her heart shatter into a million pieces. *What the?*

"Oh, hell no!"

Evie stalked out after him, pushing through the bar's door as if it were paper. Once outside, she turned first one way, then the other, looking for him. When she saw him heading toward his truck in the parking lot, she called out to him. "Jonathan Clark, don't you dare walk away from me."

He glanced over his shoulder, but continued walking toward the truck. "Doesn't feel too good, does it?"

"Oh, so now you're trying to publicly humiliate me?" He chuckled.

When Evie caught up to him, she reached out to stop him. "What's so funny?"

"Really? Public humiliation? Somehow I don't think you care what people think about you." He rocked back and forth on his heels.

"Of course I care."

"Uh-huh. Which is why you go skinny dipping on private property."

He cocked his head to the side, watching her. Then he stepped in front of her, standing so close that if Evie stepped up on her tiptoes she could kiss him.

"What are you really afraid of?" His voice was husky, filled with emotion.

Without missing a beat, she answered. "Losing you."

He stared at her, but she couldn't read his expression in the weak light from the bar's neon sign. He lifted his hand toward her face, and Evie lifted her chin upward slightly, preparing for the kiss she'd waited so long for. She had to remind herself to breathe or she was afraid she would pass out before she felt his lips on hers.

Instead of tasting his lips, she watched as he pushed a lock of hair from her face. She looked down, disappointed.

"I know you're going to run away again." Jonathan lifted her chin. "It's who you are."

She wanted to protest, but she was lost in his eyes, afraid to move, afraid he would walk away from her again.

"Make me a promise, Evie."

"Anything."

"Promise you'll always come back to me."

Evie slid her hands down his arms, then intertwined her fingers in his. "My heart belongs to you, now and forever." She pulled his hands up to her waist, pressing her body into his.

He reached around her, sliding his hands into the waistband of her pants. She jumped at the coolness of his skin against hers, then relaxed into him as he bent down to nibble on her ear. "I see that you've kept your other promise."

"Of course. Always for you."

Acknowledgments

Finding people who can tolerate all our little quirks in life can be quite the challenge, especially in small towns. Finding someone who embraces the quirks while supporting our endeavors, no matter how crazy they may seem, is a heady achievement in any environment. I am lucky to have found several people throughout my life who support me in both my quirks and my crazy ideas. I am even luckier that that the internet enables me to keep in contact with them, even when they are spread across multiple continents.

I want to take this opportunity to thank Julia Denton, who not only embraces my quirks, but also answers every question I come up with—and I come up with some real doozies. I am also grateful to Maral

Kurbanova, who helped me realize the importance of following every dream we have, regardless of how old (or young!) we are when we dream them.

Turn the page for a sneak peek at

My Heart, My Gift

A Great Plains Romance novella

Serafina Anderson stood by the baggage claim in Omaha's airport, looking for her cousin Trish Cassidy. *Trish James*, she corrected herself. She hadn't seen her cousin since the funeral for Trish's parents almost a decade ago. She wouldn't be here now if she hadn't created such a mess back home in St. Louis.

"Feeny? Is that really you?"

Sera grimaced at the nickname, but turned to see Trish, her arms spread open wide. Her cousin pulled her into a hug, and Sera noticed the talk hulking man watching them. He would have been intimidating if it weren't for the toothy grin plastered on his face.

"It's Sera, now."

Trish stepped back to look at her, still clutching her shoulders. "Now don't you get all high and mighty just because you're a college girl. You'll always be Feeny to me."

Sera scowled, ready to argue the point, but the hulking man stepped forward, one hand extended.

"Hi, Sera. I'm Dalton." As they shook hands, he leaned down to whisper, "Don't worry. I'll work on her for you." He winked, then glanced at Trish, an innocent look on his face. "So, have your bags come through yet?"

"Bags?" Sera rolled her eyes. "I'm only here for the holidays—and just while the dorms are closed."

Dalton glanced at the carry-on at her feet. "If you mean to tell me that you packed everything you needed for the next two weeks in that bag, then you need to give my wife some serious lessons."

Trish slapped her husband's shoulder playfully. "Oh, hush, and grab her bag." She hooked her elbow in Sera's and led her toward the exit. "We have a lot to catch up on, but first I want to know what's up with this?" She tugged on Sera's long black ponytail.

"It's a ponytail. By the way, did you know that there is a ponytail equation? Learned about it in physics. They use it to predict the shape of the ponytail."

"Hardy-har-har, missy. I meant the blue streak. You turning into a smurf or something?"

Sera shrugged. "I think they save transmutation for grad school."

"I'm sure your mother was mortified by your color choice."

Sera nodded, trying to hide a smile. "I'm sure she will be, when she sees it."

"Why, Feeny, you little rebel you. Next you'll be telling me you got a tattoo—oh, no! You didn't?!"

Sera ducked her head and slid in front of her cousin to walk through the exit. They hurried across the drop-off lane, bracing themselves against the icy December wind. Once they were all piled in the truck and Dalton had the heat blasting, Trish studied Sera for a moment.

"I just can't believe it. My innocent little cousin—Feeny the do-gooder, who never broke any rules—has become a rebel."

"I was nine! Nine-year-olds don't break rules."

Dalton snorted. "Clearly you don't know many nine-year-olds."

Trish shook her head, then winked at Sera. "College looks good on you."

Sera mumbled "thanks" as she shifted in her seat.

Dalton gave Sera a sympathetic smile as he whispered, "She'll stop talking. Eventually." He glanced at Trish and smiled, then looked back at Sera. "Probably about the time you get on the plane headed back home."

"Oh, you'll pay for that, Mr. James."

"I hope so, Mrs. James."

Sera pretended to laugh at their obvious teasing, but inside she was groaning. She hadn't planned to come to Nebraska for winter break, but then her best friend started dating some guy from her Spanish class and Sera had realized she couldn't spend the entire break listening to their gooey lovespeak. Trish and Dalton had been married for several months already. Weren't they supposed to be beyond all this romantic crap?

Luckily Sera was able to steer the conversation to Trish's life, so for the next few hours her cousin told her all about how she and Dalton met and how they were building a state-of-the-art horse training facility. Her cousin certainly seemed happy with her life, but Sera couldn't understand how anyone could live in a small town—or the country, for that matter—without going crazy from boredom. She wasn't sure she'd be able to last two weeks. Then again, she didn't have much choice.

Things would have been so much easier if her parents hadn't decided to go to Rome for Christmas. She could have gone home, faced the music, and then figured out what to do next. But Rome had been on her mother's bucket list for as long as Sera could remember. She wouldn't ruin that dream. When the plans with her best friend fell through, Sera had been hard pressed to find an appropriate alternative. Then she remembered hearing about Trish's whirlwind courtship and latched on to the idea of visiting Nebraska for the holidays. At least the three-hour drive to the house passed quickly, which Sera decided was a good omen.

Two weeks. Fourteen days. Surely she could last that long without getting too bored and screwing everything up? She hoped so.

When they pulled into the lane that led to the two-story farmhouse, Sera felt her determination falter. For some reason she'd pictured the farm on the edge of a small town, not twenty minutes away from any hint of civilization. The land that stretched out before them was certainly pretty, especially with the light dusting of snow over everything, but pretty would only last so long.

As they got out of the truck, another truck pulled up behind them, and two men got out. The taller of the two walked up to them with a slight smile on his face.

"Afternoon, boss, Mrs. James." He nodded first at Dalton, then Trish.

Dalton sighed dramatically. "How many times do I have to tell you? I'm not your boss."

The man shrugged. "Sorry, boss. Habit."

"Lucas, you and—is that you Andrew?" Trish stood on her tiptoes to look over Lucas's shoulder. "You and your brother come inside and have some hot chocolate with us. It's too cold to stand out here any longer."

"That's okay, Mrs. James. We'll only be..."

One withering look from Trish and Lucas was signaling to Andrew to head inside with them. Sera pretended to cough to hide her laugh. Once inside, Trish directed Dalton to take Sera's bag upstairs while she ushered Lucas, Andrew, and Sera into the kitchen.

"Guess we know who wears the pants in this household," Andrew mumbled, earning him a glare from Lucas that would have frightened Sera if she weren't so busy giggling.

They were just sitting down in the kitchen when Dalton reappeared. "So, Lucas, surprised to see you here. Didn't think my sister would give you any time off."

"She runs a tight schedule."

Dalton erupted into laughter, startling all of them except Trish, who was warming the milk for the hot chocolate.

"But we're actually here about Andrew."

Sera saw the dark look flash across Dalton's face, and she turned to study the other man. Andrew's dark brown hair and bright blue eyes contrasted with Lucas's green eyes and auburn hair. She wondered what the quiet Andrew could have done to cause Dalton's reaction, then remembered the comment in the hallway. Such comments could easily be construed as rude. Was Dalton really the kind of man to be offended when people didn't follow the rules of society?

Sera was grateful when Trish set several mugs of hot chocolate on the table. The sweet chocolate offered her an escape from the tension, if only a brief one.

"You boys can talk business later. Right now, I want you to meet my cousin Sera, from St. Louis by way of Chicago. She's a freshman in college who'll be spending Christmas with us. Sera, this is Lucas and Andrew Clark."

Andrew fingered the mug of chocolate, not looking up at Sera. "Another big city girl come to visit us uneducated rural folk?"

Sera saw the hint of a smile tugging at his lips and realized at the last minute that he was teasing her. She was about to make a similarly sarcastic remark when she noticed Lucas glaring at his brother, his lips forming a tight straight line.

Andrew must have realized his mistake because he glanced up, saw Lucas's anger, then looked around to everyone else, finally settling on Sera. "Sorry, I, uh—that didn't sound the way I meant it."

Sera shrugged. "I'll just chalk it up to the cold weather."

"Ha! You think this is cold, just wait."

"Yeah, it gets pretty cold in Chicago, too."

Andrew responded with a dismissive "bah."

"Wait, do you really think it gets colder here than in Chicago?"

"Well, you gotta deal with all the wind here. That's a cold that settles into your bones."

Sera propped her chin up on her fist. "Huh. And me living in Chicago—you think I don't know anything about wind?"

"Not like here."

Lucas interjected into their conversation, his voice so low that Sera almost didn't hear what he said. "Are you really that dense?" When Andrew frowned, the anger making his eyes an even brighter blue, Lucas shook his head. "You think they call it 'The Windy City' because of a few breezes?"

Andrew rubbed his thumb back and forth along the edge of his mug, and Sera could see him struggling to remain calm.

"Actually, with all the buildings, I rarely ever feel the wind anyway." She shrugged. "Unless I'm by the lake."

"Well, you'll feel the wind here, I'm sure." Trish stood, signaling to the mugs on the table. "Anyone need a refresher?"

"No, ma'am, I think we just better say our piece and be on our way before my brother here manages to insult anybody else." Lucas cleared his throat. "I feel bad about leaving you in a bind, what with going to work for your sister and all. But Andrew here still has a debt to work off—he did his time and all, but I believe he has a karmic debt to you. So he'd like to offer his services to you whenever you need him."

Dalton eyed Andrew for a moment, then spoke to Lucas. "That's awfully kind of you to offer, Lucas—"

"Because we could sure use the help."

Everyone but Dalton looked at Trish, who was standing behind her husband, her hand on his shoulder. Only Sera seemed to notice how deeply her hand was digging into his shoulder. Dalton's brow was so furrowed that his face was turning a mottled red.

Trish forced a smiled. "Lucas, why don't you take him for a quick tour of the place. Take Sera, too. I'm sure she'd like to see the horses."

Lucas scrambled to his feet, and Sera and Andrew were quick to follow suit. She was just pulling the front door closed behind her when she heard Dalton's voice from the kitchen, exploding in anger. She slammed the door, mumbling, "I guess the honeymoon's over." She raced down the steps to catch up to Lucas and Andrew.

Lucas was storming ahead of Andrew, glancing over his shoulder every once in a while to throw out another angry comment. "I can't believe you. What in the hell is wrong with you? When did you get to be so stupid? And being snide to someone you just met?"

"He wasn't snide to me."

The two men stopped and turned to Sera, as if just noticing that she was with them.

"That's kind of you to say, Miss Sera, but we both know my brother could use a lesson or two in manners."

Lucas continued walking to the barn, but Andrew hung back.

"I can fight my own fights. And I don't need a college education to do it." He stared at Sera, as if waiting for her to contradict him, then rolled his eyes and turned to follow his brother.

Sera stared after them, a series of retorts racing through her mind, none of which would be considered polite in any context.

an opportunity to build a ranch from the ground up. What she doesn't expect is her powerful attraction to her new boss—or how controlling he starts to become.

When Dalton James decided to build his horse ranch, the last thing he anticipated was saving a damsel in distress. Then again, Trish Cassidy isn't someone who needs saving. So why is he so protective of her? More importantly, why does he feel like he has to do the right thing around her, even when she doesn't want him to?

Heart So Sweet

With four older brothers, rancher Susannah Clark is used to dealing with men and getting them out of trouble. But when her childhood crush Tate Trudell returns as sheriff of Harrington County, Susannah must decide whether to save her brothers yet again, even if means losing the man she loves.

Tate Trudell never expected to move back to Harrington, especially after how he left things with his best friend, Lucas Clark, just before Lucas left for the war in Afghanistan. But a lot has changed in ten years, including Susannah, Lucas' little sister. When Tate discovers that her passion matches his own, he's determined to be with her. To get the woman of his dreams, he must work through his bad blood with the Clark family—if Lucas doesn't kill him first.

So Wills the Heart

When the tough gets going, artist Evie Jacobson runs away. So when her great aunt leaves her a property in rural Nebraska, Evie uses the opportunity to escape her boss, who's deluded himself into thinking she loves him. But life in the country is a bit too tame for Evie—until she meets Jonathan Clark, a man who tests the limits of her spontaneity. When Evie discovers that Jonathan might not be everything she expected, will she runaway yet again or will she have the strength to stay and face her greatest test?

Jonathan Clark's afternoon break from working the ranch turns into a fantasy-come-to-life when he encounters Evie Jacobson skinny dipping in a private pond. His water nymph's playful side excites him like no woman he's ever met, and he looks for any excuse to be with her. But a rancher's work is never done, and Jonathan must choose between his family and Evie—a woman who might have already moved on to someone else.

My Heart, My Gift

Can the big city girl convince the small-town cowboy to give Christmas a second chance? Or will the secret she hides destroy any chance of a relationship between them?

When Serafina Anderson makes a mess of her first semester of college, she does what she knows best: avoids facing her parents. This time she runs away to spend her winter vacation at the ranch of her cousin, Trish. Her escapades also lead her right into the arms of Andrew Clark, the small town's most notorious troublemaker. But Sera sees beyond Andrew's crass nature and recognizes that the bad boy isn't as bad as everyone makes him out to be.

Andrew Clark hates Christmas—at least he has since his parents died. He refuses to buy into the commercialism of the holiday and does his best to shove the hurt he feels down so deep inside him that no one will ever find it. So when Sera ignores his bad temper and rude remarks, he wonders if he's finally found the angel who can rescue him from himself—until he discovers that she's been lying to him all along.

About the Author

Corrissa James was not always a country girl. In fact, she fought it all her life, traveling the world to live in far-flung cities like St. Petersburg, Russia, Caracas, Venezuela, Varanasi, India, and Guadalajara, Mexico. She didn't realize she was meant to live in the country until she returned to her roots in Nebraska, where she discovered the beauty of the fields around her (even if she was allergic to them) and the intensity of Mother Nature (who sure packs a wallop!).

Corrissa wrote her first romance stories in junior high, although at the time she didn't really know what happened after kissing, so she improvised with lots of ellipses (…). Her professional writing career initially took her away from romance—but never far away as Corrissa could always be found with a romance book at hand.

Today she focuses on western romance novellas, offering afternoon reads focused on strong women and the men they choose (never without some struggles along the way).

If you've enjoyed this book, please leave a review.

Thank you!

Check out more works by Corrissa James and see
what's coming next by visiting
www.corrissajames.com